Paka Mdogo

Little Cat

H. S. Toshack

Illustrations by Nelson McAlister

Other books in the series:

The Gradual Elephant
The Meerkat Wars

First published in Great Britain
by
PakaMdogo Press 2009

A CIP record of this book is available from the British Library.

ISBN 978 0 9563236-0-6

A set of free teaching resources (structured in line with the UK
National Literacy Strategies but designed to help all 7-12 year old
readers explore the text fully, and extend their enjoyment of it) is
available in the *Paka Mdogo* section of the LitWorks.com website.
Go to http://www.litworks.com/childrens.php.

Baragandiri National Park is very large, and full of interesting animals, some of them also very large...and dangerous. It's not a good place to be lost in when you're very small, and easy to see (if, for instance, you're a little black-and-white cat).

The Baragandiri Map on Pages 44 and 45 will give you some idea of how big the Park is. The story will tell you what happens to the little black-and-white cat who gets lost there.

To Janet, whose eye is as sharp as Kapungu's

Contents

Chapter One: Safi

Sheena walked carefully along the gravel pathway. The small grey stones had sharp edges, and shifted and crunched under her paws; but at least they weren't as hot as the concrete slabs nearer the school would be. She'd have to stay in the shade when she got to that part of the path.

It was a very ordinary and safe pathway — first the gravel, then the concrete, and then hard brown earth winding through dark green bushes towards the School Hall; but her decision to walk along it on that sunny morning would before long lead her to some very different paths — paths less certain, paths more dangerous…

She was bored, and lonely. The housing compound where she lived was empty: all the people, grown-ups and children, had gone off to places like the beach or the ice-cream shop; and the one dog who lived on the compound (an enormous light-brown South African ridgeback called Safi) would no doubt be lying under a bush somewhere.

Safi was a Kiswahili word meaning *clean*; and Safi was a very clean dog because he never actually did anything — he was indolent on cool days, never mind hot ones — and not once had Sheena managed to get him to chase her, not even when she lay down provocatively in front of him and wiggled her short tail cheekily as if to say, 'Can't catch me-ee!' What that meant, in full, was, 'Can't catch me-ee 'cos I'll jump up a tree-ee!'

Sheena, like most cats, was very good at jumping up trees; and when she

1

found herself, a few weeks later, being chased along a rough track in a strange place, by not-a-dog-but-something-close, that particular skill would save her life…

Safi knew about cats and trees, which is why he never did more than look at her briefly with his big dark eyes and go back to whatever he had been daydreaming about – probably a field full of cats with no tree-ees around.

Because it was Sunday, there weren't even any school gardeners to annoy by scratching up the plants they'd just put in the ground. So Sheena had decided to go beyond the houses to where the school buildings were. She'd been there many times before, during the year or so she had lived at the school; but there were often lots of children moving about and making too much noise. Some of them would want to pick her up and squeeze her and she didn't want any of that, so she had always run back home as soon as someone tried.

Not that she didn't like children; but she preferred to choose the ones she was going to be squeezed by. Mainly that was Amy and Thomas, the children who lived in her house: they knew how hard *not* to squeeze a cat.

She would learn, however, once she had left paths behind altogether, what it felt like to be fully squeezed...

She walked on along the winding pathway, slowly and watchfully.

Chapter Two: Kenge

This wasn't an ordinary school. It was an International School, and that meant several things.

First of all it meant that the school wasn't in England but overseas – in Africa, in fact, although there are International Schools in most countries of the world.

Secondly it meant that the children who went to it were themselves from many different countries. Sheena had heard Thomas say that there were students of more than forty nationalities at the school, and she had seen for herself that they came in all skin-colours and had different-shaped faces and different voices. One thing they seemed to have in common, however, was that they smiled and laughed a lot, and had fun together – it was a very happy school.

Thirdly, the teachers (Amy's and Thomas's parents among them) also came from different parts of the world, and lived with their families on the Housing Campus, next to the Academic Campus…where Sheena was now headed.

When she got to the hot bits of the pathway (the concrete slabs) she walked close to the brick wall and stayed in the narrow strip of shadow at its foot until she was under the arches outside the School Library. There she stopped and looked around.

Perhaps she'd wasted her time coming here. The only person she could see was the askari (security guard) in his blue uniform with its black shoulder tabs, sitting under a large fig tree near the gate. It was his job to make sure nobody came onto the campus who had no business there; but he was asleep, with his feet up on a low wall and his rickety cane chair tipped right back. On a cooler day Sheena might have sneaked over until she was beneath the chair, and made a sudden scuttering noise with her claws in the gravel as she dashed off behind a bush to watch the chair teeter and maybe…

It was too hot for games, though, so she moved back close to the wall and rounded the corner towards the open area between the classrooms, where wide paths passed among rich, dark-green vegetation – glossy shrubs and tall, silent trees. There she stopped again, in the shade of a wall. It was a day for stopping. (Safi would have said that it was a day for not even starting.) So Sheena was surprised to see something move under a bush between her and the Hall, where the children went to what she knew were called Assemblies, big lessons where students learned to sit still and be quiet for a long time.

Cats have very sharp eyes, and are particularly good at seeing twitches in the undergrowth or up in the trees which might mean that something worth chasing is nearby. Sheena could see nothing now, however, just dappled shade under the bush. Whatever had moved had become still.

She sniffed the air, but could smell only damp heat and the musty soil on which she stood. Maybe the little movement wasn't worth investigating; but she had come looking for something to do, and she decided that she could get close to the bush without leaving the shade and going out into the open sunlight. That was important, not just because it was hot out there (she secretly hoped that this wouldn't end in a chase) but because her natural instincts were taking over, and one of the natural instincts of a cat is to see without being seen.

Sheena had a bit of a problem in that respect. She was black and white. Most of her head was black, but her face was white; the front part of her body was white, but she had black patches on her shoulders; the back part of her body was black, but her tuft of a tail was partly white, like a rabbit's.

How she came to have a tuft rather than a proper tail is interesting, but that story is told somewhere else. The fact that she had no tail to speak of wasn't altogether a bad thing, however. It made it difficult for her to balance when she was jumping, but in situations like this, where she was not jumping but sneaking, it helped not to have something long, black and white waving above her.

So what was left of Sheena's tail just moved quietly from side to side as she began stalking (sneaking, that is).

The thing that had caught her attention was well hidden. All she could see, as she crept closer, were the brown lines of branches among the dark leaves. Then there was a flat rock. Then just above the rock there was a thick branch sticking out from among the foliage. Then there were the branch's two eyes and its tongue flicking in and out.

Two eyes and a tongue! That wasn't a branch at all! A snake? If so, it was time to leave. Snakes are even better at sneaking than cats, and very nasty when they *have* sneaked.

She would have that fact, too, brought home to her forcibly, when the squeezing time came…

Instead of backing away immediately, however, Sheena became wholly still. She wanted to see more. Cats are many things, a surprising number of them beginning with 'C'. One is Choosey (Sheena was that – about who she allowed herself to be squeezed by, for instance). Another is Cautious, which is what she immediately became as soon as she saw the movement in the bushes. A third is Curious, which is what she was now being.

If it was a snake it was a very thick snake. She had seen a fat puff adder before, a sort of blotchy sausage with pointed ends (one of them very dangerous); but this was twice as big around the middle. And if it *was* a snake it was a snake with legs, she now realised as the creature slowly emerged from the bushes.

Its movements were very measured: it leaned forward and delicately placed a front foot in the soft soil. After a pause it brought a back leg forward, then its other front leg.

All the while its tongue was flicking out and in; and what was surprising was not the tongue's shape (it was forked like a snake's) nor its length (which was impressive) but its colour (bright blue). The only blue tongue Sheena had seen before was Thomas's when he'd been sucking his pen as he struggled with his homework. He'd stuck it out at the mirror when it tasted strange and had then used it to make a tongue-print on his

7

homework instead of writing his name. He got into trouble when he handed the work in; and he got into trouble at home when his mother found out why he'd got into trouble at school.

A lizard? Yes, but much larger than the creamy-coloured geckoes who hid behind the pictures on the walls of Amy's and Thomas's (and Sheena's) house and darted out to gulp mosquitoes when they settled nearby.

Now Sheena understood why she'd not been able to see the lizard clearly until she was close. It was camouflaged (another 'C' word cats like to be, but, as we've just explained, something Sheena had difficulty being). It was exactly the same murky brown as its background, and it had pale yellow circles running in lines across its body, so that all in all it looked like a mouldy, curled-up leaf with legs – a very long leaf, three times as long as Sheena from its head to the tip of the tail which now came into view as the lizard continued to move forward one steady step at a time. (It would have been only twice as long as Sheena if she'd had a proper tail.)

The lizard stepped slowly up onto the edge of the concrete path leading towards the Hall.

What to do now? Was it dangerous? Any thought of chasing it had immediately left her when she saw its size, and had been replaced by a thought of running away when she saw its teeth. They were short but very spiky – and many.

Sheena would also become quite an expert on teeth before her adventures were over...

And that tongue! It looked both inquisitive and sinister, as if it had a life of its own and was searching for something.

If the lizard itself was looking for something, it didn't really show it. It wasn't turning its head or moving its eyes. The eyes didn't seem to be focused on anything in particular. They were small and bright, but fixed, like the glass eyes of one of Amy's dolls. Sheena still felt unseen, which is how she liked to be.

Only the lizard's tongue was still moving, flickering in and out. Then the reptile slowly turned its pointed snout towards Sheena; and she knew she had been noticed. She tensed, ready to spring away backwards if the thing came towards her. How fast could it move? Geckoes were very quick, and they were only small lizards; and she didn't want to be held, wriggling, in those sharp teeth, or gulped down like one of the mosquitoes she had seen disappear as if by magic down gecko throats. She knew that some animals could be mesmerized, held in a spell, by a reptile's glittering eye, so she was on her guard against that kind of trick.

Then she was surprised again – not by a sudden movement from the lizard but by the words that came from its long slit of a mouth, words that slid out like its tongue from between its thin lips.

Cats know what they need to know. They don't usually know the time of day in hours or minutes, but they know when it's time for their food to be put on a plate and their milk in a saucer, and when someone they like is about to arrive home. They know what people are saying whenever what people are saying may affect them (for example, 'I think I'll go fishing today'), and they know when you are going away (have you never seen a cat spread itself out in an open suitcase to get in the way of the packing?)

Sheena needed to know what the lizard was saying to her; so she did know.

It was actually the friendliness of the words that was unexpected, since the lizard didn't look friendly – it was much like a snake for that.

'Hello there! What ssort of day are you having?'

There was only a slight hissing sound when the lizard spoke, as if, having grown legs and become less like a snake in appearance, he was trying not to sound like one either, since he regarded himself as being on a higher level (which, of course, he was, even though his legs were quite short).

'Oh...er...fine thanks. Just taking a stroll around, you know.'

'No you weren't, you were sstalking me, we both know that. But that'ss alright. I do quite a bit of sstalking myself, sso I can't get offended.'

'How did you know I was here? I didn't think you'd seen me.'

Sheena took pride in her stalking, and was a bit upset that she'd been caught doing it.

'Sseen? No, ssmelt you is what I did.'

'But your nostrils are so small. How could you smell me from such a distance?'

The lizard's nostrils were no more than tiny round holes half-way up his snout. (Cats are Curious, as we've already said, and they're also very observant even though that isn't a 'C' word. Call it Clever at Spotting Things, if you like.)

'Here'ss a trick you catss – you are a cat, aren't you? – could learn. Watch.'

The lizard's long blue tongue with its split end slipped out from between his lips and pointed towards Sheena for a moment, then disappeared again.

'You had milk for breakfasst, and fish yessterday.'

'How did you do that?'

'Thiss is a dual-purpose tongue I've got here – it ssmells as well as tasstes.'

'How does that help?'

'Well, your sstubby little pink nose – ssorry – can only ssmell what comes into it. My tongue goes out ssearching for ssmells, and can tell what direction they're coming from. That'ss how I knew where you were. And I knew *what* you were because my tongue carried your ssmell back into my mouth where I could get a *tasste* of it; and I knew that you were sstalking me because you were giving off a sstalking kind of ssmell, as if you were both excssited and a little bit sscared.'

'Oh.'

Sheena was annoyed and embarrassed: she'd been outsmarted *and* outsmelled; and 'stubby little' wasn't a very nice way to have your nose described.

'The only trouble with this blesssed' (that was a really hissy word) 'tongue is that it getss in the way when I'm sspeaking. Makes me ssound like a ssnake. I'm not a ssnake.

'But let'ss talk about you: what are you doing? Apart from sstalking I mean.'

It seemed that lizards, as well as cats, were curious.

'Well, I suppose I'm just looking for something interesting to do. Life's dull when my family aren't here. Come to think of it, it's not all that exciting when they are, either. I blame this place.'

Sheena looked around at the classrooms.

'My family leave home early in the morning, they don't come back all day, and when school's over they still have work to do. It seems like teachers and students spend all their time making work for each other. I don't see why they can't come to some kind of agreement about it.'

'It ssounds as if they don't have much time for fun.'

'No. I have to make my own.'

'How do you do that?'

Sheena had difficulty answering. The truth was that she didn't *have* much fun.

'Well, I – er – wander around a lot.'

'And catch thingss?'

11

'Sometimes.'

Sheena heard herself sounding rather ordinary, but she wasn't prepared to tell lies in order to be more interesting.

'I caught a crow last week.'

That was true; but the lizard didn't seem impressed.

'Oh. It would be one of those makunguru, was it, thosse black Indian crowss that have taken over down here? I hope it tassted better than the one I caught after I arrived two dayss ago. Sstupid sscrawny thing was ssitting on the ground preening itsself. I took the shine off *itss* featherss, I tell you. It was nowhere near as juicssy as the big pied crowss we have where I come from. You should try one of those if you ever get the chance.'

Sheena knew what *pied* meant. It had nothing to do with being baked in a crust. It meant black-and-white. She wasn't sure she'd find it easy to eat a pied crow: she had a soft spot for pied things, since she was one herself. She guessed, though, that once the feathers were off and fluttering away on the breeze their colour wouldn't be important. And 'juicssy' sounded good.

'Crows aren't easy to catch, though, are they?' she asked, trying to appear more knowledgeable than she really was about such things. 'Whenever there's one on the ground there are usually another ten in a tree looking out for trouble and squawking away if they see any.'

'You're right. I had to do some clever sstalking to get close enough to grab that one.'

(If that all seems rather cruel talk, well, it was only a bit of animal boasting, one predator to another like…and Sheena was rather flattered to be seen as a fellow-stalker: she'd never had to do very much actual catching of things in her easy life.)

All this time, of course, friendly though the conversation was, Sheena and the lizard had been watching each other carefully,

Sheena with her round yellow eyes, direct and unblinking, and the lizard with his colder but equally straight black stare. It was by no means a settled thing that neither would attack the other, and a tussle between them could have gone either way. The situation was nicely balanced, however, and they could therefore enjoy a short friendship instead of what might have been hostility. They were two creatures of roughly equal weight, comparably clawed and toothed, with a lot to tell each other and nothing better to do on a hot Sunday afternoon.

'Hot? No, it'ss not hot,' said the lizard when Sheena had begun to complain about the weather.

'Well, maybe it is,' the lizard smoothly agreed when Sheena started to argue. (Although she was in the shade, sunlight was being reflected from the pathway and the black parts of her fur were already uncomfortably warm.)

'What I mean is, it issn't hot for *me*. You ssee, I'm a reptile and reptiless are cold-blooded. That means that my blood never getss warm; and something which never getss something can never get *too* something.'

Sheena wasn't sure she understood all of that; but the bit about having cold blood was clear enough.

'I don't think I've ever been cold since I came to Africa,' she said. 'I'd like to have just one cool day for a change.'

Truth to tell, she had come (with her family) from the Caribbean, where the weather is very much the same; but the lack of things to do on this particular Sunday had put her in the mood which all expatriates (people who live for a while in a country different from their own) occasionally suffer from, when *nothing* works properly and *everything's* dirty and they can't *wait* to get *home*. Just where home might be for a cat of the world like Sheena is another question. But today she didn't want to be in this part of

13

Africa, where it was hot for her no matter what it was for the lizard.

'You should go up North,' said the lizard.

'What do you mean, up North? You mean to the Arctic? Only polar bears and Arctic foxes live up there.'

She had looked over, or rather under, Amy's shoulder when she'd been doing a project on the Arctic, and now she felt like showing off a bit to the lizard to get back at him for outsmelling her.

'Not sso far,' said the lizard. 'The Arctic ssounds as if it'ss a long way away. No. I'm only thinking about the North of thiss country. It'ss ssometimess cooler up there, and the air'ss clearer, and it'ss altogether a better place to be…In fact I think about it a lot. It'ss where I come from.'

'If you like it so much up there, why are you down here?'

The question when it started felt as if it was going to come out grumpy; but by the time she'd finished it Sheena realised she was interested in the answer. The lizard might not know exactly where the Arctic was, but he probably knew a lot of other things.

'It was an accsident…or rather I had an accsident…no, both.'

Sheena waited. He was obviously going to explain.

'There was thiss big truck piled high with water melonss, you ssee,' the lizard began.

Sheena knew what water melons were – massive round fruit like dark green, shiny cannonballs.

'Now I like a bit of water melon when I can get it and thiss sseemed a good opportunity: they'd loaded the truck the night before and I wass up early when no humanss were around. I climbed up a tarpaulin they'd thrown over the melonss, crawled under it and wriggled my way down where I wouldn't be sseen while I had a ssnack – a sslurp would be more accurate I

14

ssuppose: once you've gnawed your way in through the sskin it'ss more like drinking than eating. I had too much, sstayed too long, whatever, and fell into one of those dozes we lizardss are good at.

'Then ssuddenly there was a roar and the truck began to shake. The men had come out quietly and sstarted it up, and I knew I had to get out quickly. That shouldn't have been a problem – where there'ss a way in there'ss usually a way out. But the shaking loosened the pile of melonss and the oness around me ssettled downwards and ssqueezed me so that I couldn't move. Ow they were heavy! It was like being ssat on by a lot of little green hippopotamussess. They should have been called ssquash, not melonss.

'Then the truck drove off, and to cut a bumpy sstory short, here I am.'

'And here you stay?'

'Not likely. I'm off as ssoon as I can manage it. I've eaten enough csity garbage, and there issn't a lot else round here. I haven't managed to catch a good-ssized ssquirming thing ssince I arrived.'

He looked sharply at her as he said that.

Sheena's eyes widened a little. *She* was a good-sized thing and she didn't want to become a squirming one. Was that a little bit of drool forming at the corner of the lizard's mouth?

It seemed, however, that he'd just been testing her to see how she'd react: he smiled thinly when she lifted a front paw nervously off the ground.

'Don't worry, you're a bit on the big sside for me, and all that fur would get tangled round my tongue.'

'Tell me more about the North.'

Sheena wanted to keep the conversation away from eating; *and* she wanted to hear more about a different kind of Africa from

15

the dusty, smelly city that was all she'd seen in the last year.

The lizard began to talk. He talked eagerly, about the grassy savannah plains which gave him part of his name (he said his real name was Kenge, but officially he was a savannah monitor lizard. The monitor part was because one of his jobs according to the old stories people told was to keep an eye on things and give a warning when a crocodile approached – although he wasn't sure how he was supposed to do that.)

As he talked he looked off into the distance, and the one eye that was now toward Sheena gleamed; and such was his enthusiasm that she felt she could see deep in the darkness of that eye some of the places he was talking about: a flat brown land silent under a pale gold sun; gentle hills with springy grass and enough trees to allow a cat to feel safe; open skies with big dangerous birds soaring in them (she and the lizard shared a shiver when he talked about them); and shady, secret places where there were endless things to eat, some of which ran and had to be hunted down, some of which were fruit and just fell to the ground waiting to be slurped (he appeared to like that word. It seemed he hadn't had anything slurpy either since he came South).

He told stories about animals that climbed, animals that dug, animals that swam and animals that mainly just hid. He talked about animals with big ears, big eyes and big teeth, in different combinations. He described the smells of the North – he was an expert on those: the hot smell of dusty tracks, sharp fruit smells, warm nest smells, the smells of different kinds of mud. He talked about the sounds to be heard there – the growls and giggles, the hisses and howls, the roars and rattles, the whistles, whines and whispers.

The Allen family watched lots of tv programmes and dvds

about African animals, and Sheena often watched with them, fascinated (while pretending to be bored); but somehow the lizard's words made the animals seem more alive than they had ever looked on the tv screen.

'Tell me about some of the places where there are lots of things to chase.'

Sheena had not done a great deal of chasing, but she thought she was good at it and felt she would like to do more. Opportunities, however, were limited around people, who liked to get rid of most things worth running after, rats and cockroaches and suchlike.

Kenge told her, using magical-sounding names. Many of them were harsh and guttural, like Ngandogu, Gorandorogo, Kageradoma, Baragandiri, but none the less powerful for that; and the lizard spoke them throatily and with relish, as if he was proud of them. Just their sound made them seem mysterious and exciting.

'Could I go to one of those places?'

'Well, you couldn't walk there. I wass in that truck for a whole day.

'And before you get all eager to go chassing up North to look for adventures, there'ss something you need to know about the chassing game.'

Here the lizard looked at Sheena keenly, and at the same time kindly, as if he felt she needed, and deserved, some good advice.

'Thingss that chasse are chassed in their turn,' he said. There was something grim about the way he spoke, as if this was an important truth that needed to be remembered by everybody and not only by this strange little black-and-white creature he had just met.

'I know *that*,' said Sheena, unwilling to be lectured on things she hadn't asked about. But she was aware that she'd never quite managed to get Safi to chase *her,* and that really her life so far had been very safe and comfortable. Into the back of her mind came the thought that maybe there were other things to learn about chasing than just how to do it. Perhaps that was what the monitor wanted her to realise. The air seemed a little cooler, just for a moment. Sheena shivered slightly, as she had done when the lizard talked about big birds wheeling in the sky; but it was an excited kind of shiver.

'If you do want to go off on adventuress like that, Paka Mdogo,' said the monitor, 'good luck.'

Sheena was pleased to be called *paka*, the Kiswahili word for *cat* – it made her feel more African; but she wasn't too happy with *mdogo* – *little* – although she did know there were much bigger cats in places like the ones Kenge had just described with so much enthusiasm..

'As for me,' the lizard continued, 'I'm leaving now – got to look for a truck heading North, preferably an empty one.

'But before we say goodbye let me teach you a few more trickss, jusst in casse you do head off on your travelss: you probably won't be able to manage the tongue thing.' (Sheena wasn't sure she wanted to manage the tongue thing: she couldn't imagine what it would feel like to have her tongue wiggle about in her mouth like that, and the thought of it splitting at the end and becoming like a snake's made the breakfast milk in her stomach curdle.)

The monitor had spotted something coming slowly up the path towards them. It was about four inches long and black and shiny, and it was travelling on dozens of orange-coloured legs that rippled along beneath it and carried its body smoothly forward. The legs were so close together and moved so rhythmically that they were like an orange skirt hiding the wheels of a very small toy train running on an invisible track that curved from side to side. It was a millipede.

'On your way up North you might find yoursself in a place where there'ss not a lot to eat, and one of these thingss might come along. If you ate it sstraight off you'd be very ssick. It's poisonous. Thiss is what you need to do.'

The monitor stepped carefully forward so that the millipede would pass just in front of him. Then he lowered his head and touched the millipede with the underside of his jaw. The millipede immediately curled up into a tight, hard spiral so that it was like a polished black seashell. That wasn't its only defence. A sharp, unpleasant smell filled the air, making Sheena sneeze and back away. The lizard ignored the smell (although Sheena did notice that he kept his mouth firmly shut and his tongue out of sight) and began gently stroking the curled-up bug with his chin. He carried on, patiently, for quite a long time. The millipede didn't move.

Eventually the monitor gave the millipede a light tap with his claw so that it slid sideways. There was a dark stain in the soil where it had lain while he stroked it.

'There. Ssafe to eat now. It'ss used up all its poison.'

'So eat it,' said Sheena, not because she didn't believe him but because emergency rations like this had no appeal for her when there was no emergency, and she was afraid he was going to offer the millipede to her. It would have to be an Emergency, in fact, or an EMERGENCY, or even an *EMERGENCY*, before she would eat one of those things.

The lizard didn't wait for the millipede to uncurl. One gulp and it was gone, like a Danish pastry down the throat of a man with a very wide mouth who didn't believe in chewing. There hadn't even been a crunching sound.

'Er...thanks: that's really useful,' said Sheena.

'Then how about thiss?' said the monitor, and before Sheena realised what was happening he began to swell and swell so that suddenly the friendly lizard wasn't there any more. He had been replaced by a much bigger monster. Its knobbly back was humped, its throat was puffed out, it was hissing loudly and its tail thrashed angrily from side to side. Then the monster reared up on its hind legs and raised its front claws, which were very long and rattled as they opened. Its eyes pointed narrowly down at her like two glass daggers.

Sheena crouched low, feeling as if she was suddenly facing one of those dinosaurs Thomas was so interested in, a monitaurus vexed or something.

Kenge

The lizard took a step forward and Sheena jumped back — she couldn't help herself; but once she was out of reach of those curved claws she decided it was time for a little party trick of her own.

She became a very different Sheena. She arched her back until she was half as high again as normal, and raised her fur so that her neck became thicker and stronger-looking. She put out *her* claws and stood up on their points like a ballerina balanced on the tips of her toes, growled (cats can growl, although not as well as dogs: Sheena's growl sounded very like one of the place names the lizard had used — 'Gorandorogo'), then gave an even louder hiss than the monitor had done. To round off the performance she spat like fat sizzling in a pan.

The monitor fell over backwards. This startling show of aggression from an animal he had obviously thought of as tame had knocked him completely off balance. It was his turn to be embarrassed.

When he rolled over onto his feet again he seemed much shorter. His neck had subsided to its original size, his claws had shrunk and his eyes had dulled somewhat. All he could say was, 'Very good, very good.' Then he started to walk slowly off on stiff legs, trying hard to look dignified.

'Time to go! Time to go,' he sang out, looking straight forward. 'I've got a truck to catch!'

He did turn his head and look at Sheena one last time. Sheena knew what he was going to say.

'Remember, thingss that chasse…'

Then he was gone, his long body slipping quietly between two bushes.

Chapter Three: Ahali Allen

Cats are Contemplative. That's another 'C' word and it means that they *contemplate* a lot – they think about things deeply and carefully, and spend a lot of time doing it. (Cats have lots of time, as if life goes by for them more slowly than it does for people.)

Over the next few days Sheena spent a lot of time thinking about some of the things the monitor lizard had told her. She also spent a lot of time thinking about the life she led.

Basically she was a happy cat ('Contented' would be the right 'C' word to use, but not all cats are that), living with a happy family, Ahali Allen – the Allen Family – who went to or worked at a happy school. The country the school was in also seemed to be a happy, and colourful, one. The black people whose country it was were usually cheerful, and often laughed, sang and danced.

That was surprising: Sheena had heard Amy's and Thomas's parents say that the local people sometimes didn't have enough to eat, were often sick and couldn't afford proper medicine, and didn't expect to live very long. Perhaps they were so positive about life *because* they didn't expect to live very long, and also because they lived so closely together, and shared everything.

Sheena always made sure *she* had enough to eat. She made a lot of noise if it seemed like her family might have forgotten to feed her, and she had some back-up plans in case they ever did forget: she knew where other families put out food for *their* cats; she knew where the school canteen was; she kept an eye on where the birds were building their nests; and she'd sampled the insects which scuttled around, deciding which would be good to eat in larger quantities if she had to. (Her list didn't include millipedes, even after the monitor had shown her his stroking trick.)

She didn't get sick, either. She was very careful not to eat food that might not be fresh. Her nose, in spite of the rude way the monitor had talked about it, was clever enough to tell her when food wasn't safe.

As far as living a long time was concerned – she intended to, that was that.

So she was glad she wasn't one of those children who played in the dust near the dukas (the small shops lining the road into the centre of Ubanga Town), however happy they seemed. She was glad she was who and what she was, glad she lived with the Allen family, glad they had brought her here with them from the Caribbean (although the journey had terrified her)…she was all-round glad, in fact.

Still, however, the pictures the monitor had put in her mind kept coming back: pictures of landscapes where you could see so far that only the fact that the earth was round and curved away downwards stopped you seeing farther; trees so close together that you could travel for miles without touching the ground; rivers that were dry one minute and full of water – and crocodiles – the next; and strange animals of all sizes and shapes that were still and quiet most of the time but then suddenly did lots of dashing and jumping around, and often made startling noises. She wanted to see, and hear, and smell all of that.

But she wouldn't be able to, not without making a dangerous journey, not without leaving behind all the things that made her life safe and comfortable, not without saying goodbye to Amy and Thomas for a long time.

So she had to make do with contemplation…and imagination, which is all very well in its way but is a bit like looking out at a sunny day through a dusty window.

Then one evening she heard the family talking, over supper. There was a school holiday coming up and they were deciding where to go.

'Oh no!' thought Sheena. She hated to be left behind when they all went away. There was nothing to do but eat and sleep (although they were the things she chose to do a lot of the time anyway). There were no games like pretending the leather belt Thomas was wiggling under the bathroom door was a snake and pouncing on it. There was no homework spread out on the floor so that she could roll in it and crumple the pages. There was nobody to wake up during the night by sticking her nose in their ear.

She'd tried in the past to stop them going away by hiding just before they left, which meant that they had to look for her to make sure she was alright; but Thomas and Amy knew most of her hiding-places by now. She'd tried to make them feel bad when they came back, staying out for long hours and refusing to eat the food they put down for her; but people didn't remember things as well as cats, and by the time the next holiday came they'd forgotten how annoyed she had been the last time.

Some of the things they were saying now, however, made her stop grumbling to herself and listen closely. Those names – Gorandorogo, Kageradoma, Baragandiri, Ngandogu – were names the monitor had used. Was that where the family were going, up North to where life was amazing?

'A week isn't long enough to go to Gorandorogo.'

That was Amy's and Thomas's Dad speaking…and Sheena's Dad, in a way, since he was the head of the family and she was one of the family (she insisted on that). Amy's and Thomas's mother was Sheena's Mum, too; and she also was the head of the family. It all depended on what was being decided…but it did seem that Mum was the head more often than Dad.

'I'd like to go to Kibo,' said Amy, but she said it quietly and no-one seemed to hear her.

'We'd need two days to drive as far as Gorandorogo, three if we stopped off at Ngandogu. They're too far away.'

'We must go there sometime, though: they're both supposed to be wonderful places.'

That was Mum, always storing up plans for the future. Thomas, on the other hand, was always for doing things now.

'Yeah, let's go there. You could drive fast, Dad. I bet we could get there in one day if we set off really early and didn't stop.'

Sheena knew that really early wasn't a good time for Thomas, so she wasn't surprised when his parents didn't pay much attention to him.

'People have said good things about Kageradoma.'

Dad was speaking again.

'Please can we go to Kibo?' said Amy, more loudly.

'Kageradoma's a small park, it has a small lake and there's lots to see. There are always elephant around the Lodge; and someone told me the other day that the last time they were there they saw a leopard just inside the gate.'

There were some things here that Sheena didn't altogether like to hear. Park? Lodge? Gate? There was a park down the road from the school, with some old and broken children's swings in it and a rusty iron fence around it. A lodge was some kind of hotel, she thought. And gate? That meant that things were being shut in, or shut out. None of that fitted the picture she had in her mind of the Kageradoma the monitor had talked about, an open place where animals could come and go freely without being bothered, or controlled, by people.

Not that that mattered very much, since she wouldn't be going there.

Here Sheena snorted in disgust (Thomas noticed but thought she was only sneezing). That was something else her nose was good for, even if it *was* stubby and pink and little – showing her displeasure, whether it was at a bad smell or a bad idea.

You'll have realised by now that Sheena was a very sensitive cat – about her nose, yes; about her stumpy tail, a bit; but also about being left out. You may also have got the feeling that when she didn't like something she did something about it.

She had a little dark place at the back of her mind where ideas were born. She was beginning to have an idea now; but she needed to listen some more first.

'I want to go to Kibo,' said Amy.

'What about Baragandiri, then?' said Dad.

'We could probably get there in one day. We'd still have to set off as soon as it got light, *Thom*as.'

It sounded like Thomas's bluff on that one was going to be called.

'Not if you drove fast,' was Thomas's way of ignoring the awful possibility of an early start. Then he fought back a little.

'Oh, but sorry – I forgot we were going in *Great White*. Hah!'

'The roads are the problem, not the Land Rover.'

Dad was being protective of his Land Rover's reputation: *Great White* was an old vehicle of the 'they don't make them like this any more (thank goodness)' variety.

Sheena remembered the roads, even though she'd never been any further than the airport just outside the city. (She recalled the whole journey here all too well.) The roads explained why a lot of people in this part of Africa drove around in dusty or mud-splattered Land Rovers. Since teachers could afford only old models, cheerful mechanics from the area round the school were often on the housing compound with their clanging, shiny tools, lying on their backs under the silent vehicles, with anxious owners standing nearby hoping no spare parts would be needed.

'I want to go to Kibo,' said Amy once more (this time very loudly). Sheena decided it was because she was determined to take part in the discussion, and 'Kibo' was the only Park name she could pronounce.

'Let's talk to people about Baragandiri, and where the best campsites are. In the meanwhile we can start sorting out the gear.'

'The gear': he made that sound very important.

Sheena knew what 'the gear' was. Most of it was kept in a cupboard under the outside stairs. The cupboard was usually locked, which was a shame because lots of fat cockroaches lived in it. She always tried to be around when it was opened.

It was opened the very next Saturday. Two large tin trunks were hauled out and their contents emptied onto the driveway. Dad did all the heavy work, the children had most of the fun, and Mum stayed out of the way.

Sheena had some fun too, in her own fashion.

Soon there was a pile of things on the concrete (as well as a scattering of detached cockroach legs) – cooking things, digging things, tying things (ropes and chains), chopping things (a panga and an axe) and torches and lanterns of various kinds. Then there were things for the car – cans of oil, a toolbox, a tyre pump, two large plastic containers of diesel (bad smell). There were also two big canvas bags which Sheena had never seen opened. She had a good sniff around them but couldn't decide what was inside.

Sheena knew that the Allens had not used most of this before. They had never been camping in Africa and had bought most of 'the gear' from another teacher who was leaving. When they'd come back from holiday previously and talked about the places they'd stayed, it had always seemed that there had been beds, and walls, and taps and toilets and all the things people need in order to be comfortable. Camping meant living away from home without any of those.

Dad, however, was excited. He enthusiastically checked everything over, testing the lights, cleaning the tools, uncoiling and recoiling the ropes – pretending, Sheena guessed, that he knew more about them all than he actually did. He had obviously appointed himself Camper-in-Chief. He spent a long time sharpening the axe on a flat stone. It did look like he was getting ready for an adventure; and the idea which had formed at the back of Sheena's mind began to move forward, as she crunched reflectively on another cockroach too slow.

The following day the whole family got together in the back garden and opened one of the canvas bags. It was soon clear that Mum was there to organise everybody else. After a lot of unfolding and pulling around; after a lot of raising and lowering and raising again, in the hot sun; after a lot of hammering and tying; and after a lot of arguing, which went on through most of the other activities…there was a green tent with a rounded shape standing on the grass. Everybody had a cold drink. Then everybody had another one.

They opened the second bag and put up the other tent. That took them almost as long, even though the tent was identical, since they seemed to have forgotten most of the things they had learnt from putting up the first one, and the arguing was if anything louder.

It was hot and tiring work. Sheena stayed in the shade. So did Amy, this second time. Every now and again she said, 'I want to go to Kibo,' but only Sheena was listening.

Sheena wasn't around when the decision to go to Baragandiri was taken. She found out about it a few days later, again during supper. At the same time she learnt that the family would be leaving the next Saturday.

'Oho!' she thought. Her idea jumped forward.

The idea was of course to go with them. Exactly how she'd do that she didn't know, but she had always been an expert at doing things when they needed to be done, i.e. right there and then, 'Just like that'. So she didn't doubt that when the time came she'd find a way, right there and then, of going – 'Just like that'.

That was one of the (many) good aspects of being a cat. You didn't need lots of Things, so there was nothing to get ready even when you were about to leave on an adventure. Only *you* had to be ready, in your mind. And Sheena was.

By the time Friday came, several cardboard boxes with food in and two containers holding boiled water had been added to the pile inside the front door (which was where everything had been stacked ready, including the tents, now back in their bags. Taking the tents down had been almost as difficult as putting them up. Wrestling them back into the bags had been even harder: the bags seemed to have shrunk. Mum Allen simply watched this time, through the kitchen window. She was laughing. Dad Allen was not.)

Everyone helped with the loading of the Land Rover, everyone had his or her own idea about how it should be done, and everyone got in everyone else's way. It only began to work properly when Mum took one of the canvas camping chairs, unfolded it, sat down where she could see what was going on, and said, 'Right.' The other three knew what 'Right' meant, and from then on the loading went much more smoothly.

Sheena had jumped up onto Mum's lap while she gave out the orders.

'Sheena knows we're going away, as usual' (Amy).

'Don't worry, Sheena, it's only a week' (Thomas). Thomas was trying to be reassuring, and he came over and stroked Sheena's head.

'Sheena will be fine! Back to work!' (Guess who.)

Thomas more than anyone else in the family hated to upset Sheena. He didn't like leaving her, and was always anxious about her until they got home.

Little did he know that Sheena herself wasn't at all worried. Little did he know that little Sheena had a little plan (actually a big plan by cat standards). Little did he know that she wasn't on Mum's knee as a gesture of affection or even to make them feel bad about going away. She was there so that she could see into the back of the Land Rover.

She was sizing it up, or rather not all of it, just a bit of it – the bit of it right at the back, underneath the folding tables that Dad Allen, under Mum Allen's instructions, had slid in on top of the tent bags. There was a space there, a cat-sized space. If only Mum didn't have any bright ideas about how to fill it (she'd directed things very cleverly so that everything had fitted in snugly and wouldn't bounce around too much) then that might just be where a Sheena would be able to travel: not the most comfortable place in the moving world – and cats are Comfort-seeking – but a lot better than a dangerous gap among water melons as heavy as little green hippopotamussess.

She wouldn't be travelling by invitation, of course, and that was another problem – one best left until the next morning, when she'd have to rely on her sheer genius.

Chapter Four: Safari Njema

Sheena always woke up as soon as the birds started to sing. That was a good way to wake, even though the birds often interrupted the dreams she was having about birds.

She sometimes, having woken briefly, dozed a while to try and continue her dreams; but today she was fully awake in an instant. She knew she was going to have to watch very carefully what was going on.

Nothing happened quickly, however: Thomas slowed things down by not being fair.

'Come on, Thomas, you're not being fair. We're all ready, and Dad was up late last night finishing the packing so that we could leave early. Get up!'

Amy's teacher had recently given her class a vocabulary test. One of the words they'd been asked to use in a sentence of their own had been 'sternly'. Amy's sentence had been, 'Last night I had to speak to my parents sternly.' Now she was speaking sternly to Thomas.

She sounded very like Mum sometimes. Thomas probably couldn't tell which of them it was in this instance, since he had his head under three pillows and wouldn't be able to hear clearly – which is why he had his head under three pillows.

Once they'd got him up, however, and helped him a bit, he began to show signs of excitement like Amy, and was even cheeky enough to grumble when she started to change her

33

mind about which books she wanted to take with her.

'Books? This is a safari! Books? Come on, Amy. We're waiting.'

This was after their stand-around breakfast, the sort they usually had only when everybody had overslept on a school day.

Amy just humphed, and stuffed two more books into her backpack.

They all, it seemed, had some last-minute things they wanted to put into the Land Rover. Mum decided to take an extra frying pan; Dad got anxious in case the radiator boiled on the journey, and filled another water container 'to have handy'; Amy had her books (and, glaring at Thomas, crammed yet one more into her bag). Thomas was too busy deciding between his two footballs to notice her extra books or her glare, so Amy had to say something.

'A *football*? Are you going to teach the elephants to play *football*?'

All of that dithering suited Sheena just fine. The rear doors of the Land Rover had been left open, obviously so that last-minute things could be jammed in. The Sheena space was still there. For a moment she thought Thomas was going to squeeze his football into it, but then he found an empty blue bucket on the other side and dropped the ball in that so that nothing sharp could puncture it.

Mum had put out lots of cat food in the kitchen – canned food on a plate, several bowls of dried food and two big bowls of water. Sheena knew that one of the askaris would have been asked to come in every day to give her fresh food and water, but the family always started her off with plenty, to allow for a bit of forgetfulness.

Sheena ate while the family were still making their decisions. She munched steadily, careful not to make it appear that she was eating lots, even though she was. She ate much more than usual, ate more than she wanted, ate until she began to feel uncomfortably full. Then she drank lots and lots of water. She didn't know when she'd get a chance to eat or drink again.

It would have been good if she'd been able to take some food with her, and she found herself envying the little animals like squirrels and hamsters who were able to stuff their cheek pouches with snacks and store them there (or somewhere else) to eat later. She'd even tried that herself a couple of days ago, filling her cheeks with the small biscuity things she was mainly fed; but the hard little lumps had pushed her face out sideways and made it feel painfully stretched; and soon they weren't hard any more but soggy, and some went down her throat every time she swallowed. That wasn't going to work.

Safari Njema

It wouldn't be very long before she met an animal who had a very different solution to the problem of how to save food for later. That wouldn't have worked for Sheena any better than the squirrel method, however...as you'll see.

So she stuffed her stomach instead, hoping the family wouldn't notice how quickly one of the bowls had emptied.

Timing was important now – timing, and luck. Would they close up the house before they shut the Land Rover doors? Before they locked the front door of the house they would come to say goodbye to her, or at least the children would (wouldn't they? They'd better.)

She picked her moment and, carefully showing no interest in what was going on (cats are very good at being Casual), walked past them all as they stood in the driveway taking a deep family breath before setting off. She strolled into the house and jumped up on one of the chairs. A moment later Thomas and Amy came in and started to make a fuss of her. She showed no interest in that either.

'Time to lock up!'

Dad was jingling his house keys.

Amy and Thomas stroked Sheena one last time then left. Dad shut the front door and locked it. She was alone.

No time to lose! She sprang from the chair, skidded on the tiles as she rounded the doorpost into the kitchen, then burst out through the cat flap in the back door, braking only for a moment so that her stump of a tail caught the flap just when it was about to clatter shut and stopped it from making any more noise than a soft click. She raced round towards the front of the house and then slewed to a halt, peering cautiously around the corner.

This is where her luck (and she had always had lots of it) held. The back of the Land Rover was towards her, and the doors were still open. The family were grouped around the front of the vehicle: Dad had climbed up onto the large bumper – more like a shelf than a normal car bumper, as if the Land Rover had been equipped to push its way through a herd of elephants – and was leaning forwards awkwardly to polish the central part of the windscreen. Something rude must have just been said to him about his last-minute preparations, because he was obviously insisting on finishing the job and the other three were obviously insisting that he get down, get in and get off: he should never have got up in the first place, they'd clearly suggested.

It took only a moment for Sheena to jump up and wriggle down into the gap under the folding tables. The tent bag was lumpy and might feel even lumpier by the time the journey was over; but more importantly for the moment it had a large bulge which she was able to hide behind. No-one would see her.

No-one did. The rear doors were swung to, the first one with a bang and the second with a crash – she guessed that was Dad announcing the fact that *now* they could go, since he had finished his very important job. As the doors closed, the space in which she was hiding went darker. Then there was some squeaking of springs as everyone climbed in and settled down; then there was a roar as the engine started; then they began to move. She heard the metal gates open with a screech and a clang, and the askari call, 'Safari Njema! – Safe Journey!' The Land Rover swung out into the road.

Sheena was going North.

Chapter Five: Mbweha

Then they were there.

If that seems strange, remember that cats can go into trances. (Just by coincidence, one of the words for that state of mind is not just a 'C' word but a 'Cat' word – 'Catalepsy'. It doesn't, however, have to do only with cats.) Cat-trances are self-induced, as if the cat has put a spell on itself; and a cat can therefore snap out of its trance when it chooses.

As far as this journey was concerned Sheena sent herself into a trance (went cataleptic) because she knew nothing interesting was going to happen for a long time. There's nothing interesting about being jiggled around on a rough, stony road while your rear end is poked by something hard and sharp in the bag you're lying on – Sheena guessed that what she could feel was one of the things Dad Allen had hammered into the ground with a lot of puffing, to help hold the tent up. There's nothing interesting about the sickly smell of diesel when the only air you can breathe is full of it. Then there's something absolutely de-interesting about having your head bounced off a folding table every time the vehicle you're in goes over a bump...and the road North had lots of bumps and the Land Rover seemed to have no springs and the only thing protecting Sheena's head were her ears, which soon got tired of being jammed between her skull and the table, and began to droop.

So she went into a trance, and all of these uninteresting things, and the de-interesting one, ceased to matter.

She came out of the trance when Dad stopped (twice) for diesel. On a third occasion, the Land Rover pulled up by the side of the road so that the family could have a picnic, and Sheena was afraid for a moment that they might need to open the back doors to get food out; but Mum had organised things better than that.

The next time she came out of the trance things were different. There was no extra strong smell of diesel as it was being pumped. The children sounded more excited than they had been when the car stopped earlier (they'd been very quiet on the journey, as if they too had gone into trances). And there were several pairs of boots crunching on the gravel around the Land Rover, and some deep and friendly new voices.

Were they there? Was this the North? Was it Baragandiri?

She heard phrases which began to give her the answer: 'a herd of elephant', 'down by the river', 'Simba Campsite'. Then Amy spoke, and Sheena knew they were in Baragandiri.

'But I wanted to go to Kibo!'

Yes, they were here. Yes, she was here. Yes, life was suddenly going to get amazing. First, however, she was going to have to be clever, and lucky, once more.

Sheena knew that if the family discovered her there would be a problem. They would be frightened that she might run off and get lost; they would worry about the wild animals (the ones Kenge had talked about with both fear and fascination); and she knew how good people were at making rules to get in the way of fun, so she wouldn't be at all surprised if there was a notice somewhere near which said something like, 'No Bringing Your Own Animals Into The Park. You Have To Use Ours.'

So she had some choices:

1. Show herself now and hope that she wouldn't be shut in a

cage with a notice on it saying, 'Illegal Immigrant'.

2. Show herself in a few days, by which time she might at least have had some adventures and maybe managed a chase or two.

3. Try to stay out of sight for the whole week, sneak back home in the same way that she'd come and pretend she'd never been away. Then she'd have the extra enjoyment of being able to make the family feel bad for leaving her behind when she hadn't been left behind at all. Cats are very good at being absolutely nowhere; but they're equally proud of their ability to be in two places at once.

Number One was much too risky, even though she knew Thomas would make sure she had plenty to eat. A cage was a cage, no matter how good the food in it.

Number Two would be ok, she supposed, but the family might decide to cut their holiday short in order to take her straight home. She wouldn't want them to do that, in spite of her grumbles whenever they went away – she knew how much their breaks from school meant to them.

So Number Three was what she'd aim for, and if things went badly wrong and she got left behind...well there was always the Watermelon Express.

The important thing would be to stay within sight of the family, wherever they pitched the tents, and be ready when they started to take them down in a week's time.

For the moment all she had to do was remain where she was. She would sneak out of the back of the Land Rover once the family had decided where they were going to set up camp. Then let the adventures roll!

It wasn't long before the engine started up again and they moved off. The Land Rover was rattling less now, and the tyres were hissing softly, as if this was a sandy track rather than broken tarmac. That was a relief after the bumpiness of the journey.

The family had made up tongue-twisters to help pass the time as they travelled. One of Mum Allen's contributions (just after the Land Rover had bounced, jerked and swerved over a particularly bad patch of road) had been, *'Really old Land Rover relics regularly roll over on rubbly roads.'* Dad Allen, who was very proud of both his Land Rover and his driving, was not amused, and wanted to replace the word *regularly* with *rarely*. He deliberately drove through a deep pot-hole to prove her wrong and nearly proved her right.

Sheena hadn't paid much attention to the conversation during the journey. There hadn't been a lot, once they'd left the city, and most of it had been between the grown-ups. In any case she was soon in her trance. Now she listened more carefully, as the family talked about where they should camp. The Park Ranger (that was a new term to Sheena) had said they could choose between Chui Campsite and Simba Campsite. Where had she heard those names – *Chui* and – *Simba* before? Had Kenge used them?

Amy was the one who helped her with the first one.

'Chui, Chui, let's go to Chui! I want to see a leopard!'

Thomas quickly jumped in, more than likely just to contradict her.

'Simba! Simba! I want Simba! Lions for me!'

'Isn't there a Tembo campsite somewhere? I'd really like to see some elephants – friendly ones of course. Just a few would do.' Mum Allen was having her say, and she supported it with another tongue-twister:

'It would be heavenly to see eleven benevolent elephants!'

Dad explained that these were just place names, and that they were equally likely to see leopard at Simba Campsite, and vice-versa; and that they would be very lucky to see either in either place. They'd need to go further into the Park to see 'The Big Cats'.

Sheena thought that was an ideal opportunity for someone to mention Little Cats, and in particular the little cat who'd been left behind; but no-one did.

'Then let's go further into the Park.'

That was a surprise: that was Mum speaking. She was usually the one who tried to keep risks to a minimum, the one who always checked that *everything* was safe. (Dad made a show of doing that, but he sometimes missed things, and at other times the little boy in him got carried away and he completely forgot about safety.)

'But the Ranger said either Chui or Simba.'

Dad seemed to be arguing in favour of sticking to the rules. That too was a surprise: it was something he usually did only when Thomas wanted to break one.

Mum was very good at seeing gaps in rules (Thomas and Amy were learning that from her): 'But he also said we could drive around before we decided. I think if we found somewhere we preferred, we could go back and tell him, and that would be alright.'

'We don't have a lot of time before it gets dark. Remember how long it took us to put the tents up last time. And we'll have to collect wood for the fire,' was Dad Allen's response.

Dad had done enough driving for one day. He wanted to get settled; and he was probably keen to use his newly-sharpened axe and show off his newly-acquired tent-pitching skills.

Mum Allen spoke again.

'Well let's just head South for half an hour or so, then if we haven't found a good place to camp we can come back. We need to turn left before we get to that bridge down there. That must be the Ubi River. The Park Lodge is on the other side of that…and those are the Sangando Hills off to the left.'

There was a rustling and flapping of stiff paper as if Mum was looking at a map. This track apparently continued West to the campsites the Ranger had mentioned. They were about to leave it, however, and head down into the Park and away from the gate, towards…who knew what? Not Sheena. She didn't have a map.

What she had was a full bladder. What with all the water she'd drunk before they set off, all that bouncing, and now the swaying from side to side as the Land Rover set off and picked up speed on the track, she felt like an over-filled water balloon.

It just wouldn't do to let it all go on the tent bag. She was *much* politer than that; and the family would be very incensed and very investigative when they came to unload. She considered the blue bucket Thomas had put his football in, but that would give the game away as well: he was very protective of his footballs, and would make a big, puzzled fuss when he found this one floating.

So when after what seemed to her a very long time (cats have difficulty crossing their legs) the Land Rover pulled up, she thought she might just try and find a way of putting things right – she knew she wouldn't be able to hold on until they drove all the way back to the gate and from there to the campsites the Ranger had offered them. She would have to get out of the vehicle somehow.

Then the Land Rover moved off again. She had missed her opportunity. But what opportunity? Even if they had stopped longer they wouldn't have had any reason to open the rear doors; so she must hope that next time either Amy or Thomas (or both) would get out of one of the rear passenger doors. That was her only chance, so she began to wriggle forward among the camping

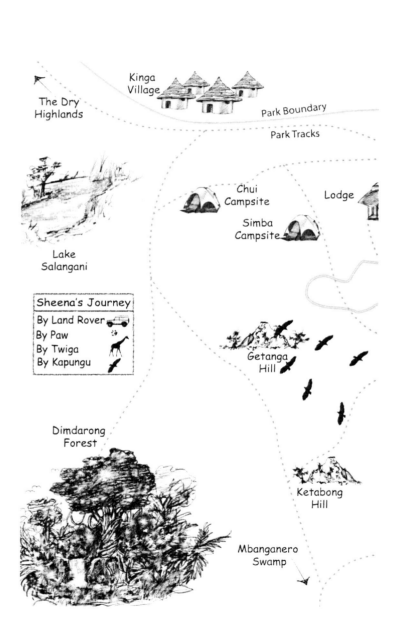

Kinga Village

The Dry Highlands

Park Boundary

Park Tracks

Chui Campsite

Lodge

Simba Campsite

Lake Salangani

Sheena's Journey

By Land Rover
By Paw
By Twiga
By Kapungu

Getanga Hill

Dimdarong Forest

Ketabong Hill

Mbanganero Swamp

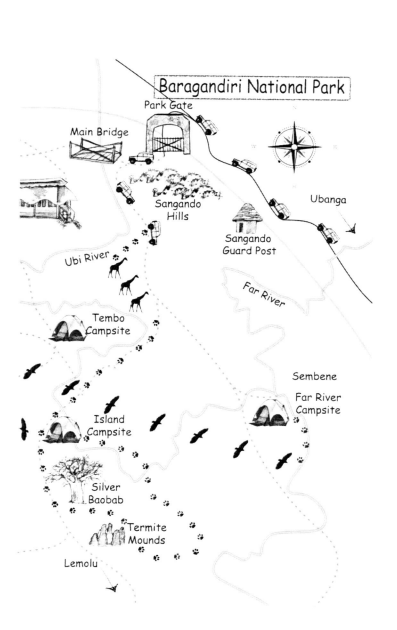

Baragandiri National Park

Park Gate

Main Bridge

Sangando Hills

Ubanga

Sangando Guard Post

Ubi River

Far River

Tembo Campsite

Sembene

Far River Campsite

Island Campsite

Silver Baobab

Termite Mounds

Lemolu

gear, past Thomas's bucket (she was sorely tempted again), between two cardboard boxes, and down the side of the tin trunks. All that squeezing through narrow spaces made her problem worse. Then she had to crawl along under the rear seat so that she was close to one side; and most of the space was taken up with a shovel and some poles. She ended up beneath Amy, and Amy started jumping up and down in excitement so that Sheena felt she was in danger of being popped in a watery sort of way by the seat springs.

She badly needed both Amy and the Land Rover to stop.

Her cat-luck came to her aid once more. Both Amy and *Great White* came to a sudden halt not much further on. Mum had seen a place she thought they might want to camp in, under some large trees. Amy was half-way out of the Land Rover even before it had fully stopped. The whole family walked back to have a close look at the shady patch of ground. They left all four doors open.

Sheena was out in a black-and-white flash, under the Land Rover even quicker, and suddenly life was good again.

Life was so good she wanted to enjoy some of its new bits before she jumped back into the Land Rover. That was a big mistake.

The family were some distance away, walking up and down under the trees. Sheena decided she had time to examine this new place, including some time to sniff (very important to cats).

What she sniffed was extraordinary. There was an overall smell of dried grass – she had never smelled grass so strongly, as if it was being baked like bread in an oven. Then within that there were many more smells, some overlaying the others, some of them like but yet unlike smells she had known: sharp catty and doggy smells, but not quite cats and dogs; smells of slithery things and hopping things; smells that were messages left by one animal for another; smells that animals had made when they were suddenly frightened.

Yet she could see no animals, and all she could hear was the discussion going on under the trees about whether the ground was flat enough to sleep on.

She stayed under the Land Rover, however. She was being another thing that cats generally are, which is Circumspect (careful to look around them, particularly when they find themselves in a new place).

She could understand why the grass smelled cooked: it was very dry, and the same golden brown as a crusty loaf. She peered forwards down the track. It curved around a bend and was then lost among more golden grass. Then she crept over to the other side of the Land Rover and found herself looking at a dog.

She was behind the rear tyre, and her immediate reaction was to crouch down so that she was less visible but ready to run if less visible wasn't good enough.

It wasn't. The dog had seen her. And it was very close, much closer than the closest tree.

'I'm not a dog. I'm a jackal,' it said; and then it was after her.

Sheena never knew how the jackal had read what was in her mind: 'Dog: not very dangerous; will pause before it runs, to decide whether it's worth the trouble; a bit slow off the mark; a bit slow in the brain also; will give up quickly; can be intimidated.'

What was plain was that the jackal had tricked her by speaking to her and giving her something to think about while it prepared its leap. What was also plain was that it wasn't slow off the mark at all: it was very quick.

The tyre saved her. She was still partly behind it, and as she turned and ran the jackal bumped into it and bounced sideways, giving her just enough time to shoot out from under the other side of the Land Rover.

If she ran straight away from the track and the jackal, however, she would be heading for the trees and the family... and they would surely see her. That could not happen. So instead she turned and raced down the side of the Land Rover, then round the front and into the long grass on the other side of the track.

The grass whipped her face as she ran. Then it thinned out somewhat and she realised she was on an uneven pathway leading away from the Land Rover.

She must keep going, must keep going, she was sure she heard the jackal (what was a jackal?) behind her, there was swishing, and panting, she was sure she heard panting. So she ran and ran, deeper and deeper into the grass, under tufts of it where they formed an arch, over tufts if she had to (although she knew that would allow the jackal to see her), and through tufts of it if there was no other way, even though that slowed her down and she thought she heard the swishing and panting getting closer behind her. The jackal would be much better than she was at dashing straight through the grass: she had seen how long his legs were.

She had also seen how big his ears were, and she knew that he would be able to follow the sound she made even if he couldn't always see her from his greater height.

Then to her left she saw a space, where the grass had had to make room for a wide bush. There was a tunnel into the bush, which was just as well since it was a thorn bush and she only just managed to get through without being spiked on the enormous sharp points.

Her whiskers helped her. A cat's whiskers are exactly as wide as its shoulders, and it knows that if it can get its head through a gap without its whiskers touching the sides, its whole body can fit through also. It would have been very nasty indeed if she'd got stuck on thorns with that dog-thing behind her.

As it was, once she was through the tunnel she knew she was safe, at least for the moment. The jackal was too tall to follow. As she turned to look back he came skidding out of the grass and stopped just short of ramming his pointed nose into the wall of thorns. Sheena was very glad to be behind them.

'Here's a pretty prickle!' she thought grimly, taking a breath before she sized up the situation and looked for something else to save herself.

The situation wasn't too bad, in fact. The thorns were in a circle around the base of a tall tree. When the jackal started to trot around the bushes, looking for a way in to her, she simply jumped onto a low branch and then scooted up the trunk until she was looking down on her pursuer.

Mbweha

The situation wasn't too bad for the moment; longer-term it was pretty awful.

The jackal might find a way in through the thorns; but then as far as she knew jackals couldn't climb (she was wrong there). Much worse was what she could see from the branch on which she now sat.

At some distance across the grass stood the Land Rover (she'd run a long way!) Thomas and Amy were just climbing into the back. The grown-ups were already in. The engine roared. Amy slammed the last door shut. They were leaving!

Sheena tried one of her most pitiful cries; then she scrabbled further up the trunk onto a higher branch and tried again. But there was no chance that she would be heard above the noise of the engine. The Land Rover drove off slowly down the track, round the bend and out of sight.

As if that wasn't bad enough, the immediate situation was getting worse. The jackal had found another gap in the thorns, and was carefully pushing his way through. She had thought he was a brown animal, but from above he was black.

'I'm a black-backed jackal,' he said, as he reached her side of the thorns. 'My name is Mbweha.'

How, again, had he known what she was thinking? He made a sort of cackling sound in his throat as if he was already congratulating himself on what would be a fine catch, and a rather silly tongue-twister, like those the Allens had been making up on the journey, came into Sheena's mind:

'Black-backed jackals cackle cruelly as they craftily catch cats.'

That didn't help at all. How much danger was she in?

Quite a lot. The jackal looked very confident, sitting back on his haunches and smiling. He scratched himself casually on his underbelly, with a rear paw, as if he was in no hurry to do

50

anything else.

Whether she could wait him out would depend on how hungry he was. She herself was well filled with cat biscuit, and the chase hadn't been long enough to make her thirsty. How patient was he? Dogs weren't, usually.

'I tell you I'm not a dog,' he said. There he was, reading her mind again. If he could keep that up, any secret escape plan she developed wouldn't stay secret for long.

She had decided that the more she found out about him the better, so she said something provocative.

'Well you look like a dog.'

(His pointed snout and big ears made him look more like a fox, actually.)

Then she tried something more provocative.

'And you've got that silly smile on your face that dogs have when they think they've done something clever.'

The jackal's eyes sharpened, but he stayed *smooth*. That was worrying.

'Let me tell you a few things before I eat you,' he said.

'Let me tell you a few things before you start,' Sheena replied promptly.

She knew it was important to show him that she wasn't afraid of him, even though of course she was. She wished for a moment that she hadn't emptied her bladder under the Land Rover, then she could have *done* something provocative and seen how he dealt with that (but squeezing through the thorns without getting a puncture and leaking would have been difficult).

'Number One: You're a dog as far as I'm concerned until you persuade me otherwise, and that'll take more brains than I think you have under your pointy ears.

'Number Two: You've got fleas' (he'd been scratching himself again), 'and I'll bet they're the same fleas that have crawled on every mangy dog I've ever known.

'Number Three: *Since* you're a dog you can't climb trees. In case you hadn't noticed, I'm sitting in one. So you may as well bug off.'

She found that she was talking to the jackal the way Amy sometimes did to Thomas, using words to make up for the fact that he was bigger and stronger than she was. Cats, and younger sisters, can be very Caustic (much the same as sarCastic).

'My turn,' said the jackal, frighteningly unruffled.

'Number One: here are a few facts about jackals and how they're different from dogs.

'We aren't choosy about what we eat. Otherwise I wouldn't be considering something as unappetising as you. Look at yourself! You haven't even been able to make up your mind whether you're black or white.'

This was clearly an attempt to demoralise Sheena, to make her feel bad about herself so that she'd jump down out of the tree and into his jaws, just to feel wanted.

Fat chance.

'When we've decided what we're going to eat, we catch it and kill it, then we hide it for a day or two so that it will taste better. Next we chew it up and swallow it bit by bit – stringy bit in your case, I should think. Then we take it back to where our pups are and we regurgitate it.'

'You re*what* it?'

Sheena didn't want to be killed, chewed up and swallowed bit by bit, but at least she knew what those words meant. She certainly didn't want to be regurgitated until she knew what regurgitating was.

'We bring the food back up from our stomachs so that the

pups can eat it.'

'Yuk!' said Sheena, and that was, 'Yuk in any case,' not, 'Yuk that might be me.' Then as she thought about it more she said, 'Yuk!' again, more loudly, and this time it meant, 'Yuk! There's no way you're going to puke me up all over the ground for little dogs to gobble up. Being eaten once is bad enough...but twice!'

'I've already chosen the hole I'm going to stuff you in when I've broken your neck with these.'

The jackal bared his teeth. The four curved and pointed ones at the front were particularly long and deadly-looking.

'Ha! I told you that you were a dog. Those are obviously canine teeth.'

That was a brave (and learned) attempt by Sheena, but the jackal wasn't impressed.

'You've never seen a dog with teeth like these!' he said, and clashed them together.

Sheena could only agree, but she did so silently. Let him read her mind again if he could.

'Dog? We were here long before dogs! There's a place a long way North of here called Olduvai Gorge where our bones have been found' (this was the jackal showing that he too knew some stuff). 'The bones were 1.7 million years old. No dogs like the ones you know lived as long ago as that.

'And we don't talk like dogs either. Listen to this.'

The jackal then emitted a mixture of loud demo sounds – howls, yelps and whines, squeaks, and some more of the self-congratulatory cackles he'd produced earlier. He ended with a series of high 'Yips' that rang out over the treetops and would clearly carry a long way.

'You might be interested in that last one,' he said. 'That's to tell my wife I'm getting take-away.'

'Sorry, Old Bones; you've misread the menu. I'm not on it.'

'Oh? Well, let's get back to your little list. As far as your Number Two goes: Yes. I've got an itch...but it's not a flea itch, it's an itch to come up and get *you*.

'Number Three: I'm not a dog I'm a jackal, as I've just proved. And here's another fact about jackals. They can climb trees.'

With that he leapt upwards and landed on the lowest branch, right where she had been when she realised the Land Rover was about to drive off. Then he stretched his body up the trunk. Stretched was the right word, since he seemed to get longer and longer until his front paws were only inches away from the branch on which Sheena now sat. His claws dug into the trunk and his back legs scrabbled away at the bark lower down. He was, as far as Sheena was concerned, the world's first climbing dog.

But she wasn't the world's first jumping cat. With a quick leap she was on the next branch up. She ran out along it and then leapt again, but not upwards this time, outwards, out over the thorn bush below, soaring until she was well clear of it and then curving downwards and landing with a dry little thump on the dusty ground.

She hadn't developed a plan, so there had been nothing in her mind to warn the jackal what she was going to do: it had been one of her 'just like that' moves.

The jackal, for all his cleverness, now made a mistake. He could have scrambled back down from the tree and wriggled out the way he had come in. Sheena would have a head (and body, and tail for what it was worth) start, but he was faster than her and knew the surrounding area. He would have caught up with her.

But he obviously thought he was a jumper as well as a climber. So he jumped; and his second error was to leap from the branch he was on instead of climbing at least one higher. He jumped from where he was. He jumped towards the same spot as Sheena. He didn't make it over the thorns.

Sheena ran for dear life through the grass, with no idea of where she was going. She did not see the jackal land among the spikes. She heard him, though. He seemed to be giving another recital of his calls, really loud this time. It wasn't all of them, however – just the howls, yelps and whines.

Chapter Six: Twiga

The birds woke her, just as they did in the city. They started singing when dawn was near; but many of the songs were unlike any she'd ever heard before. She could make out bird-shapes in the tree above her. There was an occasional flutter as wings were shaken out, and a single feather drifted down past her nose. She shifted uncomfortably on the narrow branch.

She'd decided as evening fell that another tree would be a good idea, and had found one which even she had had difficulty climbing. It had a straight trunk and its lower branches were quite thin so nothing sizeable would be able to get up to where she was. It was also very thorny (she'd had good luck with thorns the day before) and once she was close to its flat top she felt safe.

But the sounds! She'd been startled by the power and variety of the smells that surrounded her when she was under the Land Rover. Once it got dark it was what she heard that amazed her. She was at the centre of a circle of night-noise many miles across, and throughout the circle, some very far away, some terrifyingly close, some coming, some going, were animal sounds so strange that she had no idea what kind of creatures might be making them – coughs, whistles (but not bird whistles), snorts, laughs, growls (of course), whoops and screams. Once she heard a snuffling and a munching right at the foot of her tree, but she hadn't dared go down to investigate.

Did she sleep? Not a lot, not until just before the birds started moving: then there was a short time when everything fell silent. She sank into a deep and dreamless pool of unconsciousness; then the birds woke her.

The first rays of the sun stabbed at her through the leaves…and then she remembered what a difficult situation she was in.

She'd hung around cautiously on the ground for a while the night before, hoping to hear the Land Rover coming back; but it didn't. The family had either found somewhere to camp further into the Park or they'd doubled back towards the gate by another road. Either way, she'd lost them…or they'd lost her. ('Can you lose something you never knew you had?' she wondered.) So she'd climbed, then spent much of the night listening.

Now she worked her way to the top of the tree, shocking a cluster of bright yellow birds which burst upwards and scattered out of sight. She was hoping that she'd be able to get her head through into the open air and look around, but the thorns were too close together. She would have to risk going back down to the ground to find a tall tree with no thorns.

Then it was her turn to be shocked. One minute she was alone in the tree-top, the next there was a head in there with her.

And what a head! It was three times as long as Sheena's whole body, with enormous dark eyes, two short furry horns with black-tipped knobs on the end, large ears that pointed upwards, and wide lips that curled outwards. She could see nothing of the animal to which she assumed the head was attached. She couldn't understand how it could have reached so high (or did heads just float around in the air up North, and poke themselves into trees?)

'Hellooo. Who are yooou?'

This animal made its words last a long time.

'I'm Sheeeeena.'

It was catching: Sheena felt her own words slowing down.

'Twiiiga. Nice to meet you; but *what* are you?'

'A cat.'

Sheena kept it short this time.

'Oh.'

Suspicion.

'Nothing to do with those other cats, I hope, those liiions and leeeopards – the Big Cats.'

The head was suddenly withdrawn, as if the animal (if there was one) had felt a need to look over its shoulder (if it had one). Then it came back through the hole again, and moved nearer to her as if the head's owner wanted a closer look.

'I don't think so,' said Sheena. 'I know they're cats too...but they're a very different *kind* of cat.'

Sheena had noticed that lots of animals (and people, for that matter) were very anxious to be differentiated from other animals (and people) that looked like them. The monitor lizard had made it quite clear he wasn't a snake; and the jackal had wanted to be known as *not* a dog almost as much as he had wanted to eat Sheena and sick her up again. Here she was, now, wanting to be known as *not* a Big Cat. It seemed as if this animal had problems with Big Cats.

Sheena had a problem with Big Heads, particularly if they had Big Teeth (although she hadn't seen any here yet) so she was being careful.

'I hope I'm not blocking your view,' said the head.

'I was just passing by and I saw something black-and-white moving among the branches. You don't live in here, do you?'

'No. I don't live around here at all. I'm just passing by as well. I needed somewhere to sleep.'

When you're in what may be another animal's territory it's

always a good idea to say that you're just passing by.

'Sleeping in a tree...I've sometimes wondered what that's like. I often wonder what sleeping's like, in fact – proper sleeping, I mean. All I can manage are a few minutes at a time.'

'Why?'

This wasn't just curiosity. Sheena was employing the find-out-more-about-them-than-they're-finding-out-about-you tactic. You never knew when something you had learnt by asking the right questions might help you in (or out of) a difficult situation.

'Well I can't lie down flat for one thing. All the blood would rush to my head and my brain might burst. I have to lie with my head on my legs, and that's uncomfortable.

'Then there are the cats. The Big Cats that is. They'd love to catch me napping. I'm not a fighter, you see, I'm a runner-awayer; and it takes me a long time to get to my feet...so I can't afford to fall really asleep.'

So the head must have a body, Sheena thought, and legs, and feet. But it was a long way to the ground from here: was this twiga thing standing on a ladder?

'Well *I* didn't fall really asleep last night either. You lot make an awful lot of noise after the sun goes down.'

'Us lot? Not us, not twigas. A bit of grunting and snorting, that's all we do, and sometimes, on a bad day, a little moaning...like you're doing yourself right now, if I may say.'

Sheena didn't like to be thought of as a moaner so she changed the subject – to what was a more important topic anyway.

'You're not blocking my view. But would you mind telling me what you can see out there?'

'Out here?'

The head was withdrawn again but the voice continued.

59

'Usual stuff – grass and trees.'

'Any sign of a Land Rover...er...a big white car?'

'No. Why?'

'I've lost one.'

Sheena had faced up to the fact that she was the one who had done the losing, and she was the only one who could put that right.

The head came back in again and its big eyes looked at her with curiosity.

'Oh. I'm beginning to see. You came here with *people*.'

'Yes, I'm a domestic cat – a people cat.'

'A domesticat? I've never heard of those. You've lost your people and you want to find them again?'

'Yes. But I really need to find them without them knowing. I'm not supposed to be here at all, you see. I got chased last night and had to jump up a tree (not this one); and they drove away.'

'What chased you?'

'He said he was a jackal.'

'Jackal? Nasty snapping things. I had to kick one once because he got too close to one of our calves. He flew through the air and ended up in an acacia – a thorn tree like this one.'

Here, then, was another fact about jackals: they weren't very good at staying out of thorns.

'Tell you what. I'm off for a stroll. Why don't you come with me and we'll see what we can see.'

A guide might be useful, Sheena thought.

'Thank you very much. Hang on and I'll climb down.'

She turned, ready to climb carefully down the tree trunk.

'No, *you* hang on – here.'

The enormous eyes were fringed with extremely long eyelashes, and the twiga flicked them upwards so that it was clear that he wanted Sheena to climb up onto his head.

Sheena kept her claws in, stepped delicately up onto the twiga's forehead, then turned round slowly and jammed herself down between the furry horns, bracing her paws against the bony lump between his eyes.

'Hold on tight and keep your head down!' said the twiga, and

Sheena was pulled out through the hole like a cork from a bottle, but without a 'Pop!' – there was plenty of room – and more importantly without a scratch.

When she saw where she really was, she nearly fell off. What she did do was almost worse than that would have been. She dug her claws instinctively into the bony lump on the twiga's forehead.

'Ow! Careful!' said the twiga, and he tossed his head backwards.

Now none of this was deliberate: Sheena wasn't trying to hurt the twiga and he wasn't trying to get rid of her. They'd just taken each other by surprise. The result however was that Sheena lost her grip and began sliding down the twiga's neck.

'I'm sliding!' was all she could think of to shout.

'I'm inclined to think you're right,' said the twiga.

'It's *because* you're inclined that I'm sliding,' said Sheena.

And it was a *long* way down the twiga's neck. That was what had started the whole thing. Sheena had found herself sitting on a head, but she knew about that. What she hadn't known was that the head would be on top of a neck as long as a tree trunk. The shoulders which supported the neck were massive and sloped steeply down towards the animal's tail, which was also long and finished in a tuft of bristly black hair. That wasn't the end of it (though tails usually are). The whole body stood on legs that were as long as the neck, that is to say very long indeed. When you added it all up Sheena was many metres off the ground. It was as if she had stepped from the top branch of one tree onto the top branch of another, one with legs.

She had begun, while she was still inside the tree, to suspect what this creature was; and now she knew. A twiga was in fact a giraffe; and this was a very large giraffe.

She slid, and slid, all the way down the neck, all the way down the back, all the way down the tail. She was about to dig in with her claws when she realised that might make matters worse. There was no way of stopping the slide. She just managed to catch hold of the black tuft at the end of the twiga's tail. She swung from side to side like a clock pendulum, feeling silly.

'What *are* you doing? Come back up here.'

'Can't,' said Sheena, 'not without sticking my claws into you, and you obviously didn't like that the first time.'

'Let go then,' said the twiga.

Sheena wasn't sure about that: she was still quite a long way from the hard-looking earth beneath.

'Oh, wait a minute,' said the twiga, and turned so that his tail, with Sheena still on the end, was hanging down into a tall tuft of grass. Sheena released her grip, twisted her body as it rustled down through the grass, and landed with only a slight thud in the middle of the tuft. When she climbed out she was covered in grass seeds, and sneezed.

'Here you go,' said the twiga, and he started to bend down so that Sheena could climb back onto his head.

But it wasn't as easy as that. Because his legs were so long the twiga had to splay them out slowly on either side before his head got anywhere near ground level. Sheena still had to give a little jump and balance carefully on his forehead. Then she settled back where she had been before she started to slide, and the twiga raised his head again, up, up, up to the level of the treetops.

'That bending down looked painful,' Sheena said.

'Is that what you have to do every time you want to drink?'

'Yes it is; but at least we don't have to drink too often. We can go for a whole month without water: we get most of the liquid we need from the leaves we chew.'

'So you...er...don't eat animals?'

(She really meant small animals, with a particular interest in small black-and-white animals.)

'Heavens, no.'

Sheena guessed that 'Heavens' was an especially meaningful term for the twiga, since he almost lived there.

'Sorry about scratching you like that.'

'Sorry about shedding you like that,' replied the twiga. 'Your claws tickled rather than hurt. That lump you're leaning on is mainly bone. We males grow bumps on our heads so that we can bash each other with them.'

'Why on earth' (Sheena had decided earth, not heaven, should be her point of reference, since she was doing a lot of landing on it with varying degrees of thump) 'do you do that?'

'Oh, to prove how tough we are in front of our females. Though they seem to think the fact that we choose to bang our heads together to impress them is proof enough in itself that our skulls are thick.'

'Sounds like a game of bonkers to me,' said Sheena, but she didn't think the twiga got the joke. When he told her later that female giraffes give birth standing up and that the babies fall onto their heads, she decided that might explain this strange male behaviour she was hearing about.

'Well then, where should we go?' asked her transport.

'I don't know,' Sheena said. 'I have no idea where my family went. They were heading South last night.'

'South it is, then,' said the twiga; and he started to walk.

Sheena nearly fell off again. The twiga had a most peculiar style of walking. Most animals lift only one leg per side at any one time; but the twiga lifted both left-side legs, put them down, and then lifted both right-side legs. That meant he rocked from side to side as he moved forward, like a ship. It really was a stroll, or rather stroooll, since it was very leisurely, like the twiga's speech.

'You do walk funny,' Sheena had to say, as she tipped gently one way then the other.

'I'll have you know this is a very efficient way of moving,' said the twiga. 'It has to be. Our hearts already have to work hard just to keep the blood pumping up as far as our heads.'

'But why do you have such a long neck anyway?'

'Goes with the legs.'

Sheena didn't think the twiga was talking about fashion accessories, and she was right.

'People tell all kind of stories about how we came to be like this. The simple answer is that the best food's near the top of the tree, and over many, many years as we stretched up to grasp it with our tongues we gradually outgrew other animals. They have to make do with what they can reach further down. So we have hardly any competition up there: only elephants can reach that high...and they cheat of course. They use their trunks; and when they can't quite get to the juiciest leaves they just snap the branch off. They say elephants are smart but I'm not always sure.

'Here's an even better bit. Because male twigas are a yard taller than female, we can eat at the very tops of the trees; so males and females never get in each other's way when it comes to feeding. How about that for family planning?'

Sheena didn't think that was what family planning meant; but that did seem to be a good eating arrangement. She was all for not having to share food with others.

This was the beginning of some long conversations they had as they moved through the Park in the early morning sunshine.

They had not been travelling long before a line of darker vegetation appeared off to their right.

'That's the Ubi River,' said the twiga. 'It winds Southwards through the first part of the Park. Beyond those trees there's a place where people sometimes camp, but it's on the other side of the river, and there's no way across here. We'll come to a track soon, one your people may have gone down. Then all we can do is stay close to it and hope that we'll see them.'

As they moved onwards Sheena learnt lots about twigas. Their other name, *giraffe*, came, the twiga explained, from an Arabic word and meant *one who walks swiftly*.

Sheena hadn't thought they were walking swiftly: the twiga's long, rolling strides were steady rather than speedy; but she did notice they were covering a lot of ground. The clump of trees where she had spent the night was already a long way behind.

'I prefer the Ethiopian word which *giraffe* is also connected to,' said the twiga.

'It means *graceful one*.'

Sheena, too, thought that was better. They had recently passed several other giraffes in the middle distance, walking in the opposite direction, and their movement had indeed been graceful. Some of them did stop suddenly when they saw one of their own with a black-and-white lump on its head. Sheena wondered whether they were other males, startled by what might turn out to be a secret weapon for use in the bonkers war, but they needn't have worried: there was no way she would sit still and allow herself to be clonked against other giraffe heads.

'Then there's the other name – *camelopard*. That's what the Greeks called us and it means…'

'Let me guess,' interrupted Sheena, who thought she already knew the answer.

'It means *camel dressed up as a leopard*.'

The giraffe's coat had a very marked pattern.

'Well done!' said the twiga.

Sheena thought this name was a useful one also. For all its gracefulness, the twiga did have a most odd appearance, as if it was a mixture of animals and had been designed by a committee like one of those teacher committees the Allen parents often complained about.

This animal certainly *worked*, however. They had travelled quite a distance in a short space of time; they could see a long way, so they knew when everything was safe up ahead; and Sheena had been surprised twice by other giraffes standing in tree-shade. Their light-coloured coats with dark, irregular patches had made them difficult to see until they were quite close.

'I'm actually a Maasai giraffe,' Twiga had told her. (By this point 'the twiga' had become 'Twiga'. He had started calling Sheena 'Paka', and she liked the sound of that, just as she had done when Kenge used the name.)

'We're the only kind of giraffe in these parts.'

At one point they stopped so that Twiga could eat. Sheena had to hang on tight (without using her claws) because as he stretched way up towards the tree-tops, his head tipped up also so that it was in a straight line with his neck, as if he had a special neck joint. Sheena was in danger of ending up swinging from his tail again.

Once she was sure she wasn't going to fall, she watched how he fed. She knew she was going to have to learn a lot to stay safe in this dangerous place, and she was very ready to pick up a few ideas.

There was nothing to help her here, however, even if she had wanted to eat thorny trees. Twiga had a very long, purplish-black tongue, and he wrapped it around the twigs with the newest and greenest leaves. Then he pulled his head back so that his tongue stripped the leaves off. The thorns didn't seem to bother him — he had a very leathery mouth; but they bothered Sheena, who came close to getting spiked a few times.

She was beginning to feel a bit hungry herself. She had had a drink from a muddy pool some miles back, but there had been nothing to eat there. She considered asking him to lower her to the ground now so that she could scrabble around in the undergrowth in the hope of chasing out something edible.

Just then, however, there was a fluttering behind her. She turned her head and looked down towards Twiga's rump. A bird had landed on it. It was a rather ordinary-looking brown bird, apart from its red beak. It was within cat jumping distance, but Sheena was facing the wrong way. Carefully (and with difficulty, since Twiga continued to eat and his head and neck were almost vertical) she turned around and lay back down, this time facing back towards Twiga's rear end...and towards the bird sitting on it. The bird was poking about with its beak in the giraffe's coat. Sheena's memory of a tail twitched as she prepared to spring.

'Hey! Don't do that!'

Twiga had stopped eating. He had suddenly realised what Sheena was up to.

'That's an ox-pecker.'

'Good — I'm feeling ox-peckish,' said Sheena, and got ready to spring once more.

'No! We need them! They pick our ticks off for us.'

Sheena was annoyed. This was her first chance to actually catch something in this place where life seemed to be all about catching without getting caught. And the bird apparently knew it was safe: it was hopping up along the giraffe's spine towards her.

Sheena snorted as she turned around again to face the front.

Pesky ox-peckers perpetually picking ticks off tree-tall twigas should be sent packing!'

Then as she settled down between the giraffe's horns ready for the next part of the journey, she complained again.

'It's all very well protecting my food from me – I suppose you think that's what's meant by keeping your pecker up – but I'm hungry.'

'Sorry – maybe you can get down for a while next time I stop.'

They set off again. Sheena turned her head after a short while, and felt a little itch in her claws when she saw how far up Twiga's back the bird had come; but it soon flew off.

By now they were well into the day; and well into the Park, Sheena estimated. Twiga had told her that they would soon join the track South – their main hope of finding the Allens.

The landscape was mainly dry grassland – elephant grass, Twiga said, and Sheena wondered whether that was because it was very tall or because elephants were to be found in it or because elephants ate it – or all three.

She hadn't seen any elephants yet. In fact she had seen far fewer animals of any kind than she had expected. In the videos she had watched alongside the family there were animals everywhere, and they were always doing dramatic things like getting eaten.

Every so often they came to a clump of trees, many of them thorny acacias (*flat-tops* was another name Twiga gave them), and the giraffe stopped more and more often for a long nibble with his long tongue and rubbery lips. He explained that he usually spent half his day feeding, and a further third chewing what he had eaten. He called that ruminating, and it involved bringing food back up from his stomach (which had four compartments), chewing it for a while and then sending it down again to get digested some more.

That was a bit like the jackal's trick, and almost as yucky (although not so very different, Sheena thought, from chewing gum).

The Allen children were *never* allowed to chew gum. So Thomas always took his out when he was going to have to speak to his parents. If he had to do that unexpectedly he hid the gum quickly by sticking it in strange places – on the end of his pencil, for instance (pretending it was an indiarubber: once he'd even managed to carry on chewing it while he did his homework, as if he was gnawing the end of his pencil to help him with a difficult maths problem. Chewing and thinking did seem to go together, which is why people said they were 'ruminating' on something when they were turning it over in their minds, and why animals that chewed grass – cows for instance – could seem much more philosophical about life.)

Sheena remembered all too well the time Thomas's father had suddenly sat down beside him to help with his homework. Thomas had slipped a piece of well-chewed gum out of his mouth, reached down to where Sheena was lying peacefully at his feet under the table, stuck the gum in her fur and given her a hard prod with his foot so that she ran away. He didn't ask for it back, and it took Sheena a long, long time to lick it out of her fur.

Now she thought how much better it would have been if he had learnt to swallow his gum and bring it back up again when the danger had passed.

'Look,' said Twiga, interrupting what had become slightly sentimental memories of her life with the Allens: she was missing them. Where were they?

'Look there,' said the giraffe. Sheena saw a sandy line beyond the next cluster of trees, winding off over a low hill.

'The track.'

At last! Sheena stood up in excitement, wobbled, and had to sit down again. Maybe if they followed the track they would come across two green tents under some trees, and there would be a fire and the smell of food, and the sound of Amy's and Thomas's voices, and things would start to get better again. Maybe that would happen soon. Night wasn't very far off and she didn't want to spend another one in a tree. Who knew what kind of head might be in there with her when she woke up?

But events took a different turn, as if they too were on a winding track.

There was a sudden noise on the far side of the trees, which were still quite a way off. It was a pitiful noise, half way between a bleat and a moan. Immediately Twiga stiffened (Sheena found herself even higher in the air); immediately he began to run, saying nothing.

Now Sheena saw why he was called swift in Arabic. No longer did his hooves lift on alternate sides. Once he got up speed he galloped more like a horse, bringing his back legs in front of his front ones and driving forward, back legs then front legs then neck, as if a great ripple were passing through his body at each stride. Those strides were enormous, with a lift and a pause between them, and it seemed that he was running in slow motion. That was only an illusion. He was moving over the open ground very rapidly indeed, and his hooves beat on the hard earth with a sound like an African drum: 'g-dung, g-dung.' Sheena could also feel the thumping of his heart: it made his whole body reverberate like an even bigger drum: 'g-Dung! g-Dung!'

He was moving so fast by the time they reached the trees that as he went round them he had to lean into the turn and Sheena felt herself beginning to slide sideways. Her claws came out automatically to help her keep her grip; but Twiga didn't seem to notice. He had recognized the cry.

There was a terrible sight just beyond the trees. A young giraffe, a very much smaller and lighter-coloured version of Twiga, was standing still in an open space. It was doing the bleating. On its back crouched what Sheena knew was a leopard, its claws digging into the giraffe's back. Blood was trickling down over the lovely star-covered hide. Even worse, the leopard had bitten deeply into the giraffe's neck (which was much thinner than Twiga's) and was gripping there with its teeth as if nothing would ever shake it loose. The young giraffe was helpless, and trembling violently. Its great dark eyes rolled backwards as if it felt a need to watch this awful thing that was happening to it.

Sheena looked at the leopard, and was stunned. For she was staring into an enlarging mirror, at a great cat with ferocious teeth and vicious claws, intent on killing. Yes it was a very different colour, and a very different size; but that was all. In the leopard she recognised herself.

In that instant another understanding came to Sheena. A game park wasn't a place where you played games. A game park was a place where you either lived or died, depending on how big, how fast, how strong, how clever or how lucky you were. And she was a part of all of that, and had been even before she came here.

She also understood in an instant that this giraffe calf was going to be killed.

But an instant was all it took for Twiga to reach the spot.

'I'm a runner-awayer,' he'd said; but he had shown himself to be a runner-towarder as well. He skidded to a halt, raising a cloud of dust and snorting angrily. Then he reared partially up on his hind legs (Sheena had to grab again) and lashed out with his front hooves.

Sheena hadn't looked at his hooves till then. They were

massive, and split in the middle as if they were designed for walking on soft ground. And they were very heavy-looking, as if they were also designed for knocking leopards off young giraffes' backs.

That is what they did. They caught the leopard thwunk in the ribs and lifted him, spinning, high into the air. He twisted just before he hit the ground, landed on his paws, and scrabbled with his claws in the loose dirt as he began to run. As he ran he turned his head and snarled; but he didn't stop. He didn't stop until he had disappeared deep into the long grass. Then Sheena could follow his progress by the shaking of the grass stalks and the snarling, which went on for a long time as it receded into the distance.

Twiga stood very still, watching the spot where the leopard

had disappeared until there was no doubt that it had altogether gone.

'Very strange, very strange,' he said, more to himself than to Sheena, and as he spoke he walked over and nuzzled the young giraffe as if to reassure it.

'Chui do not usually attack young giraffe. Babies, yes, but half-grown animals – no, no. There is much hunger among the Big Cats, I have heard.'

This young giraffe was in a sorry state. Blood was running down its neck now, where the leopard's teeth had sunk in. Twiga continued to nuzzle it. Sheena was still in place between his horns, and didn't like to be brought so close to those dreadful wounds. She could smell the blood that was trickling from them.

The young giraffe had not stopped trembling.

'Will it be alright?' Sheena couldn't help asking, even though she knew the calf's future was very uncertain indeed.

'All depends, all depends,' said Twiga.

'The bleeding's not a problem in itself, although we bleed hard because our blood pressure's so high. It'll stop soon. The smell of the blood, though, that *is* a problem. Every animal within a mile will have heard what happened here, and some of them will have set off already, following their noses. They'll want their share of whatever's going…

'So *we're* going. We have to get away. I know an old acacia forest where we can hide and where some of the worst animals will have difficulty reaching us.

'But that's the end of your ride I'm afraid, little Paka. And I'd advise you to get as far away from here as possible. They'll be here soon.

'Just follow the track. Good luck.'

As he spoke he had been slowly splaying his legs and lowering his head, and Sheena knew it was time to get off. She took care not to extend her claws as she stepped out from between his horns. Once she was on the ground she looked around, fearfully. She wasn't exactly sure who 'they' were, but she knew what they'd be interested in, so she had no intention of waiting around to see which animals might suddenly appear.

She watched the two giraffes closely as they loped off towards the sunset. The last she saw of Twiga was his great head, coloured pink by the low sun, rocking out of sight beyond the trees.

Sheena was strangely pleased to be back on her own four paws, even if it was in a world that had suddenly become much less friendly than it had seemed just a brief while ago. Now it was a matter of how far her paws could carry her in a very short time. So she began to run; and she ran South.

Chapter Seven: Manyani

Things which are terrifying can also be beautiful. Sheena was thinking about the leopard.

She was unhappy to be related to an animal which had tried so cruelly to kill the young giraffe; but she had also felt a secret pride in its power and its perfection. It had looked so *strong;* and its coat had been so *rich*, with markings like neat black paw-prints in golden sand. She could picture the coat clearly even now, and the leopard's square shoulders and upward-curving tail…but she could also see its teeth in the giraffe's neck, and hear its ugly snarl as it ran away. Life was such a mixture!

She was sitting up in a tree once more. She had run along the track through the first part of the night, stopping and crouching down only when she heard strange noises. She had done lots of stopping and crouching.

On one occasion it had been profitable crouching. While she was stilled in the grass at the bottom of a low mound, she heard a sound different from that of the galloping hooves that had caused her to hide that time around. It was a rustling, and it was coming down towards her from the top of the mound. It wasn't a big rustling, so she waited as the noise and whatever was making it trickled nearer.

Soon a little nose poked through the grass in front of her. It was recognisable as a mouse nose, and it was sniffing. Sheena had done her own sniffing, and the smell that came with the sound was approximately a mouse smell. So she pounced. And she ate. And as she sat in the tree this morning, part of her thinking was that as far as the mouse was concerned she had been as great and as terrible and as sudden as the leopard had been to the giraffe calf.

'Oh dear,' she thought, 'I'm getting very philosophical. I'll be chewing grass next.'

She didn't mean chewing grass instead of chewing mice. Cats eat meat, that's all there is to it; and she had felt Carniravenous (she thought that was the right word) as she travelled.

It was dawn on her second full day in the Park. How many days did she have to find the family? Four? Five? They had planned to return home before the weekend so that they were back in plenty of time to get ready for school on the following Monday. Thomas no doubt would have some last-minute homework to do (all of his homework was last-minute) and Amy would be missing her friends. Sheena hoped they would both be missing her.

Her plan was simply to keep going, with hope. What else could she do?

She worked her way down from the branch she'd eventually climbed up onto when she was too tired to run any more, and set off once again.

She continued to follow the general line of the track, but cut some of its corners: it seemed to wander a lot.

There were various tread-marks in the sand, but none of them looked exactly like *Great White*'s. She tried sniffing them, but she knew that one tyre smelt very much like another, and there was no trace even of Safi in any of the indentations.

One stretch of the track looked very much like another, too; but its line was a bit straighter here. She decided to stay on it for a while.

Now she missed Twiga and his graceful legs. It took her a long time to get to the next bend, and even longer to the bend after that. More to break the monotony than anything else she tried walking the twiga way.

She just couldn't get it right. After a lifetime of moving her legs one at a time she had great difficulty persuading the two on her left side to move together, then the two on her right side. Even when she began to succeed she didn't think her success was worth very much: she was rocking from side to side like a carved wooden animal with fixed joints, and making very little forward progress.

She was concentrating so hard as she (very slowly) rounded the next curve that she didn't see the creature sitting in the track ahead of her until it spoke.

'What's wrong with you? Don't your legs bend? Looks like you're trying to remember how to walk. Either that or you've peed yourself.'

That was a rather rude comment, Sheena thought; but then it came from a rather rude-looking animal, with an appearance as unattractive as its voice. It was a very big monkey with an ugly dog's head. ('Committee at work again,' Sheena thought.)

It was sitting up in the dust, but its arms were long enough to rest on the ground. It didn't look ready to spring, so Sheena stopped and waited to see if it had anything more or less to say – more interesting or less rude, she didn't mind which. If it was neither she planned to walk by in a dignified way (cat style not twiga style) and not look back.

A combination of things made the dog-monkey seem insolent. Its pushy manner was matched by a very pushy face, one that came forward aggressively into a long snout with wide nostrils at the end. Its eyes were bright, small and close together, and set back under a forehead with a straight bottom edge as if there was a much smaller animal in there, looking out from under an overhanging cliff and watching Sheena suspiciously.

No more suspiciously than she was watching it. She had nearly been caught already by an animal which had begun by engaging her in conversation to throw her off guard.

'You can't come through here walking like that. In fact you can't come through here at all, not without paying a toll. This is a Manyani road.'

'What do you mean, a toll?'

'You have to give us something that will be useful to us.'

Sheena couldn't see any usses around, but that didn't mean there weren't any. The grass on either side of the track was long.

'Who's *us*?'

'Us manyani – baboons if you like; baboons if you don't like; and *we* don't like strangers, especially strangers that look like little Big Cats.'

Sheena was tempted to give him back a bit of his rudeness and point out that he was getting his sizes mixed up, but she decided to be unprovocative in case he wasn't getting his numbers mixed up as well and there were lots of him.

'What can I possibly have that will be useful to you?'

'Information of course. We need to know stuff. That's how we survive, by knowing everything that's going on around here. Then we can't be taken by surprise.

'Tell us where you've been and what you've been doing.'

Sheena decided that if it was a story he wanted he could have one. She could give him a tall toll tale about riding on a giraffe's head. So she told him about Twiga and the leopard (she decided to keep the jackal story in case she needed to pay another toll sometime).

Unfortunately she got a bit carried away at the end and started being philosophical again about how the leopard had excited her in spite of the awful thing he was doing. That seemed to anger the baboon.

'So you *are* one of them, you pied pygmy! You've been sent to spy on us!'

He gave a loud two-note bark – 'Gwahoo!' – that made Sheena jump ('He's a dog after all!' she thought) and in no time there was a crashing in the long grass on both sides of the track and several more baboons came bounding out into the open. Sheena was surrounded.

They all looked alike, with coarse olive-green fur and straight, thin-lipped mouths. They stared at her very piercingly from under their beetling brows. They had pulled their ears back so that the skin on their faces was stretched tight and their teeth began to show. That made them even uglier.

'What have we got here then?' said the largest of them, in a voice just as rasping as the first baboon's.

'Spy. Cat spy.'

'Oh-ho!' said the big baboon, and yawned.

It wasn't a bored 'when will this lesson end?' sort of yawn, or an 'I need fresh air somebody please open the window' yawn. It was a 'look how big my canine teeth are' yawn. They were enormous, larger than the jackal's, larger even than the leopard's.

The baboon's jaws opened so wide that Sheena could have jumped in, and his glistening yellow fangs were like the teeth of a spring trap ready to clash together…around Sheena's head, he was obviously suggesting.

He seemed to be in charge. These young male baboons were ranked according to which tribe they had come from originally, who their mother had been, how big they were, how good they were at fighting, how many young females they had managed to make friends with in this tribe, and so on...not very important things as far as Sheena could see. Cleverness didn't seem to come into it much, at least judging by this fellow. He took a long time to decide what they should do with her, and that involved a lot of running round in circles. Sheena reckoned he was doing a lot of running round in circles inside his head also.

She found out all about this ranking business over the course of the day. For she became the baboons' prisoner. That was very frustrating for a little cat who badly needed to get on. But the baboons were sure she knew more than she was saying (which was just about right, since she was saying nothing) and made her come along with them to join the rest of the troop so that they could ask her more questions.

One good thing was that they were heading down the track, in what seemed to be roughly a Southerly direction.

She had difficulty keeping up with the group. They seemed to be in a hurry to get where they were going, and galloped along without pausing on their thick rubbery legs, steering themselves by pushing on the ground with the knuckles on the end of their long arms. They stayed on all sides of her, so there was no chance of escape. The big baboon ran on ahead.

She decided to be a bit troublesome. She suddenly stopped running (the two baboons immediately behind her had to pull up sharply, didn't do a very good job, bumped into each other and fell over). She then began to walk the twiga way, first one side then the other. That slowed her right down, as well as making her look silly once more.

'What's up, then?' asked the big baboon belligerently when he had stopped and come back to where they were.

'That's how it was walking when I found it.' The original baboon had come back as well.

'Why are you walking like that?' asked the big baboon. He was clearly not pleased at the delay.

'Sorry. Every so often I forget how to walk and have to learn again. It's because I was dropped on my head when I was a kitten. Running's out of the question until I get these legs sorted out.'

'Forgotten how to walk?' said the big baboon. 'Let me help you remember.'

He yawned again.

Sheena suddenly remembered how to walk, and even how to run.

The only other good thing about the journey was that their speed brought them quite quickly to where they were going. Around yet another bend in the track (there had been lots) they all slowed down, and Sheena saw a strange sight.

Ahead of them, walking slowly along the side of the track, was a smaller baboon than the ones who had captured her; and on its back, sitting upright like a jockey on a horse, was a baby baboon. It looked just a bit like Amy out on one of her riding lessons – a little bit proud, and a little bit tottery. The top of its head, covered in velvety black hair, even resembled Amy's riding helmet.

One major difference however was that the baby was pretty ugly – very ugly and not pretty at all, in fact, although Amy would have probably called it cute (words like *cute* and things like chewing gum were among the outcomes of attendance at an International School). The hair covering its pale skin was thin and straggly, and bare patches showed through. Its naked ears were large and pink and had straight edges – they looked as if they had been cut out of cardboard with large scissors and carelessly stuck on, too far back on the sides of its head. Its eyes were small and recessed so far under its large forehead that they could hardly be seen. Its skinny little body had knobbly knees and elbows.

'Disastrous child,' Sheena said – to herself.

Then she realised she was in the middle of a large group of baboons all moving steadily in the same direction. There were other mothers carrying infants on their backs; some mothers had very young, dark-coloured babies hanging underneath their stomachs and were supporting them with one paw, which made walking more difficult; and there were lots of young males running around the outside of the group. Most of Sheena's captors joined them. Up ahead on rocks, hillocks and tree-stumps were several very big baboons with grey in their fur and large ruffs around their necks. These older baboons, continuously looking around, would wait for the group to reach them and then jump down and move on ahead to find another vantage point from which to check for danger.

When you put all the parts together it was a very efficient and safe way for the troop to move. Sheena had no choice but to fall in with them and keep going: two large louts had stayed at her heels.

None of the larger group spoke to her, nor even looked at her. It seemed that the troop could concentrate on only one thing at a time, and for the moment it was travelling.

They stopped twice, in clearings, to forage for food, and once more at a small, stagnant pool where Sheena had a long drink of water with a very brackish taste. Still no-one showed any interest in her apart from her two guards, who watched her out of the corners of their eyes (she knew because she was watching them out of the corners of hers).

These stops gave her an opportunity to look more closely at this strange group of creatures she had, against her will, become a part of.

Many of the females had bare patches on their rear ends, some much redder and shinier than others.

'Bit rude, just like the way they talk!' Sheena thought.

Their feeding consisted of grubbing around in the dirt for anything edible that had fallen from the trees. They also dug up roots from the ground and chewed them. One baboon (Sheena thought he had been in the group which caught her – she was beginning to distinguish some individuals) turned over a stone and picked up what to Sheena's surprise was a scorpion. She knew how poisonous scorpions are; but the baboon just nipped the scorpion's tail with its remarkably clever fingers and picked off the sting, then crunched the rest in its teeth.

Some of the baboons were obviously stuffing their cheek pouches, and gradually became fat-faced; but looking at what they were eating, which was mainly scraps of things, Sheena couldn't understand why they needed such horrific canines.

'Waste of good teeth,' she thought.

Then she saw the teeth in action again, and she changed her mind – not just about the teeth, but about how well the baboons got on with one another.

There was a sudden burst of noise and rising dust on the other side of the troop, and two young males came racing through, screaming, and scattering mothers and babies. Sheena saw one youngster who had been sitting daydreaming on his mother's rump (she wasn't sure afterwards that he hadn't had his thumb in his mouth) lose his balance, fall over backwards and end up in the grass as a heap of bony arms and legs with a frightened face on top.

One of the male baboons was chasing the other. They'd obviously fallen out about something.

The baboon in front suddenly stopped and spun round to face his pursuer, opening his mouth wide. His formidable fangs were like curved ivory daggers dripping with saliva (and fear, Sheena reckoned). The other baboon stopped and bared his teeth also. They were clearly into a 'you-show-me-yours-and-I'll-show-you-mine' sort of game, but a very serious one.

They circled each other, jaws wide open like that, for several moments. Then the one who had been chased must have decided he was a few millimetres short of what was needed, lost his nerve and turned to run again. In a flash the other was on him and they tumbled over and over in the dust, snarling and snapping at each other.

'Just like dogs!' Sheena sniffed.

Then the first baboon broke free and did a very strange thing.

All of the other baboons had by now got out of the way and were standing watching. Among them and close to the fighting pair was a young mother with a very small, black baby clinging to her underside. The baboon who was getting the worst of the encounter rushed over and snatched the baby.

'Oh no! He's going to swing it by its knobbly little legs and bash the other baboon with it!' Sheena thought.

She'd seen Amy do that once, with her favourite doll, Annie, when Thomas had really really annoyed her. What really really *really* annoyed her was that when she thwacked Thomas on the head, Annie's head came off. Luckily, Thomas's didn't. (Sheena thought 'game of bonkers' then too.) Thomas picked up the doll's head and dropped it in the toilet. Amy only just managed to stop him from flushing it.

Sheena really really really didn't want to see the baby's head come off in this fight (*'Baby baboon's black bonce gets bonked off in belligerent bruisers' brawl'*); but that's not what happened. Instead, the male baboon cradled the baby in its arms and rocked it back and forward as if trying to soothe it to sleep. Sheena wouldn't have been surprised to hear him break into, 'Rock a Bye Baby'.

As he did this he looked slyly over his shoulder at his opponent; but the other baboon had all at once lost interest, as if the one who was cuddling the baby had suddenly turned into a cissy who didn't deserve any further attention. The winner, for that is what he now was, turned his back and walked off, stiff-armed and self-satisfied.

As soon as that happened the baboon with the baby dropped it (on its head, Sheena noticed: it might grow up peculiar like the male giraffes, or it might forget how to walk when it got older) and scampered off in a very different direction.

Once the baby's mother had picked it up and hung it underneath her again (it hadn't even whimpered) it was as if nothing at all had taken place.

The fight had ended because the loser had sent a signal to the winner which said something like, 'Don't want to fight no more thank you very much I have this baby to look after you see.'

Amy and her friends had signals like that for when they wanted time out from their noisy chasing games: they shouted, 'Flinch!' and crossed their fingers; or they stood on one leg; or they touched a special tree. The baboon had picked up a special baby (was it because it was very small and very black?) to escape being hurt. Good trick!

The baboons spent a lot of time sending each other signals like that. This became apparent when they stopped for the night, at a place they called 'Island Campsite'. (Sheena looked around hopefully for tents, but there were none.)

A clump of very tall trees stood in the middle of a river bed running at right angles to the track. The river was very nearly dry, so they could reach the trees without getting wet. From up in their branches they would have a good view of the whole area around them.

Some more foraging went on around the base of the trees, but there wasn't much to eat there and in any case most of the baboons seemed more interested in what Sheena could only describe as nit-picking. They paired up, and one of each pair began searching its partner's fur — for fleas, she guessed, or maybe ticks. Ox-peckers might have agreed to keep giraffes clear of ticks, but they probably wouldn't help these nasty untrustworthy creatures, so the baboons had to help each other.

Sheena had never had a tick on her, but knew what they were – little blood-sucking insects that got much bigger as they filled themselves from the veins of animals they had grabbed onto and bored into with their sharp proboscises. 'They start off flat and then they get fat.' She knew that much.

Just watching all this picking and scratching made her feel itchy. Maybe she had collected a tick or two herself in the long grass. She began to nibble through her fur in the itchy places. There was one spot she couldn't reach, however, between her shoulder blades, and she twisted around, trying to get there with her sharp little incisors.

Then she suddenly felt fingers plucking at the fur on her flank.

'They've come for me!' she thought. She'd been waiting for that.

But she wasn't being attacked. The hairs on her side were being pulled apart and teeth not her own were gnawing at her bared skin. What a strange feeling!

Her instinct was to jump forward from the probing fingers, then to turn and hiss in anger; but something held her still. Maybe it was the gentleness of the fingers. Maybe it was the feeling that she was not in any danger. Maybe it was the fact that many of the animals around her were having this very same thing done to them. It was like a nightly ritual before sleep; and she was part of it; and it was not at all unpleasant. In fact it was very nice. So instead of jumping and hissing, she said, over her shoulder, 'Oooh yes…down a little bit…left a little bit. That's it. Lovely!'

She remembered her friend Toby in the Caribbean. He was a big, grey, easygoing tabby cat who every now and again would give her a quick lick to let her know that he wanted to be licked back. Licking back as far as he was concerned however was being licked back *lots*. He seemed to know that once he had stimulated the licking response in Sheena he could just lie there and enjoy it. It had all been very one-sided (although Toby had insisted that he was well and truly licked on *both* sides).

This grooming was one-sided too, but for once Sheena was on the right side.

'Thank you,' she said when the picking and nibbling seemed to have stopped, and she turned to see who had been doing it.

A young female baboon was standing nervously behind her (slightly hunched over and looking away, avoiding Sheena's eyes). Perhaps it was her nervousness which explained the gentleness, that and the fact that unlike the males she didn't have a great set of shiny fangs to make the nibbling difficult.

'Thank *you*,' said the baboon.

'It's very lonely when you have no-one to groom.'

Grooming, that was it. Amy did it to her pony. But she used

special stiff brushes, not her fingers and teeth.

'Why don't you join in with the others?'

'No-one wants to groom me; and no-one will let me groom *them*. That's because I'm a very low-ranking baboon.'

Her eyes were still moving restlessly across the landscape as if she didn't feel she deserved to look another animal in the eye, even a strange little animal like the one in front of her.

'What does that mean, *low-ranking*?'

'Well, my mother was never very important. She was always sick and had difficulty keeping up with the troop whenever they moved. Then she mated with a stranger from another troop who turned out to be very good at being no good at anything except being no good at anything except... He was my father. Then my mother died, while I was quite small.

'Since then no-one has taken any interest in me, not even the young males who come round from other tribes looking for young females to protect as a way of joining this one. I can't walk well either, you see, and I'm always being left behind. One of these days a leopard will find me by myself....

'I'd almost forgotten how to groom. Did I do alright?'

The baboon was desperate for approval. Sheena didn't have much time for animals that felt sorry for themselves or were anxious about public opinion. Being a cat, she'd always been used to making her own way in the world without worrying about what other cats thought of her – or people, or big stupid dogs for that matter.

Toby, however – well he had been different. She had cared what he thought; but he was a friend, not an audience, and when he died she had missed him badly (not, though, because he thought she was great at licking).

He had died from an illness called cat leukemia. It wasn't only in Africa that things jumped on you out of the darkness.

This baboon was a sad little figure, however, and partly out of kindness Sheena started asking her questions about her life in the troop. (If she'd been really kind, she supposed, she could have tried grooming the baboon in return, but the thought of actually ending up with a crunchy little blood-filled tick between her teeth put her altogether off that idea.)

Grooming seemed to be very important to all the baboons, which is why this poor soul was so upset at being left out.

'Grooming is our way of telling exactly who we are. It's all a matter of who grooms who: there are strict rules. And if you don't groom at all you don't exist.'

Sheena had heard the Allen parents talk about how people scratched each others' backs as a way of getting things they wanted; but this baboon stuff was Extreme Grooming.

The other reason why she had begun to ask questions was of course to discover as much as she could about these animals. She needed to get away from them as soon as possible. Why were they keeping her here?

Soon after they had stopped, the big baboon who had brought her had come and demanded once more to be told what she had been up to – his assumption seemed to be that cats, big or small, were always up to something. She'd told him about the Allens and the lost Land Rover, but that story didn't seem to interest him since there were no leopards or lions or cheetahs in it. Since then she had been left alone. The two guards were still close by, but they had paid no attention while Sheena was being groomed. All of the baboons spent a lot of time looking *away*, as if looking *at* someone was likely to cause trouble.

She didn't find out what the baboons wanted her for until the next morning.

Chapter Eight: Dunzi

'So we need you to be a dunzi for *us*.'

The baboon speaking was the biggest and oldest in the whole troop. A dunzi was a spy, he had just explained.

All of the older baboons were grouped around Sheena, staring at her intently. She stared back. She was in a bad mood because she'd been made to sleep on a spiky branch in a lower part of one of the trees; and she was in a bad mood because she wanted to get on with her search for the Allens, and now these scruffy dog-monkeys clearly had other plans for her. In addition, she didn't like being called a dunzi.

Lions were not usually a problem for baboons. They stayed out of each others' way; and if their paths did cross the big male baboons were so good at ganging up and making a lot of threatening noise and showing a lot of threatening teeth that the lions usually ran off.

There'd been a change, however. A young female baboon and her baby had disappeared from the tail end of the group when it was on the move. The outrunners – the young males whose job it was to protect the troop – had realised something was wrong when they heard a scream from behind. They had been careless and allowed the mother to drop back; and when they ran to investigate there were only the smells of lion and terrified baboon to tell what had happened.

Two days later one of the highest-ranking members of the

troop had gone on ahead to find a new sleeping spot for them. He hadn't returned; and the other senior members of the troop eventually found a flock of vultures under an acacia tree tearing with their great red beaks at the raw remains of his body.

The vultures had flapped off heavily as the baboons approached, and settled with a crash in the trees nearby, bending the branches. They would be back.

There were lion claw marks on the skull and its thin covering of shredded fur, and the lion smell was unmistakable.

'Why is this happening?' the old baboon had asked Sheena angrily. A tuft of white bristly hairs stuck out between his eyes and made him look even fiercer than the other baboons.

'How should I know? Ask the lions.'

'You should know because you are a cat, and all cats think alike. If you *don't* know then you must go and find out.'

'Ok,' said Sheena.

She wanted nothing better than to be sent off on an errand. But the old baboon was ahead of her on that.

'I suppose you think there'll be no need for you to come back? You think you'll be able to scamper off, do you?'

Scarper off is what Sheena had in mind.

'No, no! Very willing to help! But how do I find the lions?'

'They're up ahead, the only pride in this part of the Park. You will go and spy on them – however you choose. You can pretend to be their long-lost stunted cousin from Black-and-White Land for all we care.'

Sheena didn't like 'stunted'. 'Black-and-White Land' didn't sound so bad, and she wondered if there was such a place.

'And here's why you'll come back. When you do, and if you've found out something useful, we'll tell you where your friends are.'

A lot of talking had clearly gone on in the higher branches of the trees last night. Sheena wished she'd crept up there and listened.

'How do you know where they are?'

'We know everything that happens in the Park. Most of our young males are originally from other baboon troops, and there's always a lot of coming and going. Another troop has seen your precious Land Rover.'

'I don't believe you do know everything. There are some things you don't seem to know at all – for instance what goes on in Big Cats' minds. Otherwise you wouldn't be sending me to find out.'

'But we think we know what goes on in *little* cats' minds, and we know you'll do what we say. You have no chance of finding the Land Rover without our help – do you realise how big the Park is?'

Sheena did realise, sort of, and knew she was caught, and would have to do what the baboons told her. But she was also anxious. How could she spy on the lions without getting *really* caught, and chewed? She had no illusions that a group of lions, if they were hungry, would spare her because she said she was a long-lost cousin, stunted or not. She just had to hope she would find a way of dealing with that problem when it arose.

So it was that Sheena set off down the track again, with instructions from the baboons about where to find the lions.

Chapter Nine: Nygwasi

The baboons had told Sheena to follow the track towards an area they said was called Lemolu. (Sheena asked if there would be road signs, and the baboons looked at her suspiciously as if they couldn't quite make up their minds whether she was being cheeky, i.e. Cheeky. She was; and she thought for a moment they were about to start yawning at her.)

After a while she would see a cone-shaped hill off to the right of the track – 'Ketabong Hill', they called it. While that was still in sight she would come to a large silver baobab on the left-hand side, with no other trees near it.

'What's a baobab?' she asked.

They decided that this at least was a serious question, but in her opinion they didn't give her a very serious answer.

'It's an upside-down tree.'

That wasn't a helpful description; but Sheena wanted to get on with things and didn't press for a better one.

The tree would have a large stork's nest in its upper branches. (Would the branches be under the ground? Sheena wondered but didn't ask.) One of the troop's patrols had heard lions off to the left from there the evening before, but they weren't sure how far away the pride had been. When lions roar at full volume they can be heard for eight kilometres, but they also have the very strange ability to roar *softly*, and a lion that sounds as if it's away in the distance may be just past the next bush. The patrolling baboons had taken no chances and had pretended the sun was lower in the sky than it actually was.

'Time to go home!' had been their common decision, and they had loped off back towards the troop, looking behind them with their shifty eyes as they travelled.

Sheena found the tree after what seemed a long time. She was anxious, as she trotted steadily along the road with the sun rising higher and higher, about how long all of this was taking. Today was Tuesday, she had worked out. If the Allens were going to leave the Park early on Friday, she had less than three full days to find them…or, more precisely, less than three days to find out 'something useful' from the lions, take it back to the baboons and persuade them to tell her where the Land Rover was – and then get there.

'Upside down tree' was a good description after all. The baobab was easily recognisable. It was much bigger than any trees she had so far seen in the Park, and had a massive, straight trunk with a silvery-gold sheen to it. Its branches were odd-looking. They started only at the top of the trunk, were bare, and spread out into a network of smaller branches, then twigs that were more like fine roots. It wasn't hard to imagine the real branches buried underground, with leaves and maybe blossoms on them, and perhaps even a bird or two singing muffled songs in the musty darkness.

The stork's nest, however, was in a sensible place – in the open air towards the top of the tree. Sheena wondered at the size: it was more like a platform than a nest. It was so large that she couldn't see whether it was occupied, even though she knew how big storks were. They must feel very safe up there when they were at home, she decided; and they must be able to see a long way.

For the first time in her life Sheena found herself wishing her body was different (although she had often regretted the loss of her tail). She wished she had wings. They would make her present predicament so much easier: she'd be able to flap up to the nest and use it as a look-out point. She was sure she'd be able to see the Land Rover from up there. She couldn't climb up – the trunk was too vertical and smooth for that. Only wings would do it. She wouldn't mind if they fell off afterwards.

She didn't have wings. All she had was the Lion Option. So she turned left off the track and moved carefully through the scrub.

She had slowed to a walk by now. She walked and walked. The sun was sinking in the sky behind her by the time she reached some scattered trees and decided she had to rest. Had she missed the lions somewhere?

As she passed into the shadows under the trees she heard faint but curious sounds coming from beyond them – grunting and popping. They didn't seem to be dangerous sounds so she crept forward cautiously until she could see past the last tree in the clump.

Five chunky little animals were standing side by side in a row, all facing the same way and with their backs to Sheena. They had obviously just finished responding to what Dad Allen would have said was 'a call of nature' and Thomas would have called something different: the poppings had been caused by droppings. Sheena, unfortunately, was down-wind of them and she found her little pink nose wrinkling, and her eyes watering.

All five now began kicking dirt around as if they wanted to cover the evidence, but they were doing it very carelessly, thought

Sheena, whose toilet habits were immaculate.

They were strange-looking creatures. There was something dwarf-like about them. Their heads were very large and long and hairy. Their shoulders were smooth and muscular, but their bodies were rounded and quite small, and sloped away to short, spindly legs. The feet on the end of the legs were tiny.

They also looked as fierce as dwarves. Their jaws were square at the bottom, and curved tusks grew out sideways from their mouths. Their faces had lumps growing on them, in pairs. Their eyes glittered.

'Warthogs,' Sheena said to herself.

Warthogs were a kind of wild pig. She knew they ate only what they could find in and on the ground – grasses, roots and fruit. So they would not be interested in her as food; and she was not large enough to be considered a threat. That was just as well: she remembered a video in which four warthogs chased a leopard that had tried to grab a warthoglet. They caught it and tossed it high in the air, then trampled it.

That was what those ferocious tusks were for – protection. Sheena would have felt protected too if she had lived behind a pair of curved spikes like that. Their rear ends were protected, too, she had discovered: her eyes were still watering.

'Er...excuse me.'

She had stepped out into the open. The warthogs stopped their scattering and turned towards her, lining up sideways so that they were shoulder to shoulder once more. They peered at her as if their eyesight wasn't very good. They seemed nervous, and she thought it would be a good idea if she let them have a good look at her so that they realised they had nothing to fear from her. So she strolled casually past them and examined the distant landscape before turning back and speaking again. They watched her carefully throughout.

'Excuse me. I'm looking for some lions. Have you seen any?'

The warthogs turned sharply and trotted off.

'Most helpful!' said Sheena, to herself once more.

The warthogs stopped, turned, and looked at her. Then they trotted off again. They held their tufted tails straight up in the air above their shiny little bottoms and ran in a tight, business-like way as if they had important things to do.

But Sheena had important things to do as well, and these were the only animals she had seen since she left the baboons, and she needed help – so she wasn't going to let them get away so easily.

She set off after them, not trying to catch up (they looked like they would be able to outrun her easily) but staying at a distance behind them which she hoped they would see as respectful.

They stopped again, looked back at her, and trotted off once more.

This happened several times.

Eventually they halted under some trees and began snuffling in the ground. Some of them knelt down and walked around on their knees, pushing their snouts through the short grass. Even the kneeling ones watched her carefully while they fed, however. The fact that their eyes were set very high on their foreheads allowed them to do that easily in spite of the fact that their heads were lowered.

Sheena walked slowly up to them.

'What were you doing back there, when I saw you first of all? Why were you standing in a row?'

She knew the answer all too well, but showing some interest in them and their affairs might be strategically better than talking about lions.

'Poop stop.'

'Nygwasi always poop like that.'

'It's very social.'

'Keeps us regular, too.'

'Ten times a dayers, we are.'

'Always on time, always on target.'

That made it sound as if they were proud of their performance, and were in some kind of sports league. Did they play matches?

'Do you do other things together?'

'Eat together.'

'Sleep together.'

Sheena realised that the warthogs were taking it in strict turns to speak; and no warthog was allowed to say more than one thing at a time. That probably made them all feel equally important (feeling important, and looking important, seemed to matter to them).

That broke up the conversation terribly, however; and having to look from one speaker to another to another to another to another in quick succession, round and round, made Sheena quite dizzy.

'Practise fighting together.'

'We're a team.'

Sheena's suspicions were confirmed. They probably called themselves the Whiffy Warriors or the Baragandiri Blasters or something. Perhaps the Gassy Nygwasis. (*When the Gassy Nygwasis get goals galore their fans in the grandstand gasp.*)

'And travel around together?'

'Course.'

'So in your travels, do you ever see lions?'

'Course.'

'See 'em and stay away from 'em.'

'That's the only way to deal with lions.'

'Have you seen any today?'

'Nope.'

'Did we see any yesterday?'

'Nope.'

This wasn't sounding too good.

'What do you want with lions?'

'I need to find out something useful from them.'

'The only useful thing you need from lions is information about where they're going next so that you can go somewhere else.'

It was plain to Sheena that wherever the warthogs were (in this case, right here) the lions wouldn't be. But in order to stay away from something you have to know where it is, as had just been explained to her. So she persevered.

'Do you have any idea where they might be now, though?'

'Last we saw of them, they were East of here.'

'And a little bit South.'

'Looking for zebra.'

'Waste of time.'

'No water, no zebra.'

'Tough times, these, for the big animals.'

'How far away to the East?'

'*...and a little bit South.*'

(The warthog who'd said that originally clearly wanted his contribution recognised.)

'Pretty long way.'

'One day.'

'Maybe.'

'Maybe less.'

'Maybe more.'

One day! That was one day there and one long day back to the baboons then perhaps one day to the Land Rover. Too far! But Sheena was too tired to travel on tonight; and she needed these lively little animals to help her if she was to find the lions.

'Do you mind if I stay with you tonight? I'm a bit frightened of the dark.'

'So you should be.'

'Round here.'

'We never go out at night – do we?'

A series of 'Nos', 'No Fears' and 'Not On Your Knuckly Kneeses' went round the circle of warthogs.

'Guess we can find a hole for you.'

'Later.'

'Things to do first.'

One of the things they had to do, it seemed, was line up again for team practice. Sheena quickly left them to it.

Soon they trotted past her in their busy fashion. There was a word to describe their bottoms, Sheena decided. It was 'pert' – a mixture of 'perky' (as in 'slightly cheeky', a very appropriate word for bottoms) and 'smart' (as in, 'Don't you think I look very smart?')

She followed.

She was relieved to note that they were heading in the right direction – East (and a little bit South, she assumed); but she knew they would be going nowhere near the lions.

They stopped and fed again before long, near a very muddy pool from which Sheena had to drink whether she liked it or not. By now it was dusk, and she was worn out: the warthogs had trotted briskly. Her heart sank when they set off once more. But this time they did not go much further before stopping.

'Here we are.'

They turned towards her as she caught up.

'This is where we spend the night.'

'We're right in the middle of our home range.'

'If there were any lions around we'd know about it.'

There was a cluster of mounds near a large tree. They were like very tall, pointed sand-castles, but sun-baked and hard. Several of them had holes at the base.

'Old termite-mounds.'

'Good to sleep under.'

'Keep you warm.'

'Keep you safe.'

'Yours is over there.'

Sheena realised that the warthogs had formed a circle which included her. Their conversation had now become even more formalised: it went round the ring clockwise and everyone was expected to add something. It was now her turn.

'Thank you.'

That started another round.

'Don't mention it.'

'Glad to help.'

'But we don't like lions.'

'Why do you want to find...'

'...Lions?'

Number Five had finished Number Four's question for him. This was like a game of pass-the-parcel, and the trick was to avoid being caught with nothing to say. 'Committees,' Sheena thought.

'I need to discover why they've been eating baboons.'

She couldn't match the warthogs in a brevity competition any more than she would be able to compete with them in the pooping league. But at least she wouldn't be caught with nothing to say. She had a long story to tell.

She told it. She decided that was the only way to get them to help (beyond offering her shelter, which they had already most kindly done).

She told it once they had settled into their individual burrows for the night. Each warthog backed into a hole at the base of a termite mound, and stopped with its tusky snout sticking out forwards. The mounds were in a circle so that the warthogs could all see each other.

Sheena had backed into her hole too, but she only had a whiskery face to block the hole with and didn't feel quite so well defended.

Telling the story was a slow business, however. Every time she got to the end of a sentence the warthogs started a round of comments and she had to wait till her turn came again before she could continue.

She tried making her sentences as long as possible, but that didn't altogether help. They wanted all of the details, and kept taking her back to bits she'd just finished, urging her to add more. It seemed as if story-telling was an important part of their life. What else was there to help pass the time when you were stuck in a hole from sunset to dawn every night?

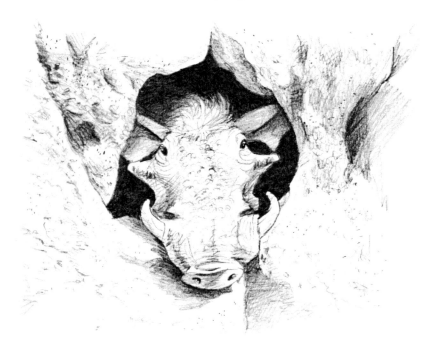

They allowed her only one pause. When she had told them about Twiga rescuing the young giraffe and described the pair of them rocking off into the sunset they had wanted to know whether she thought the youngster would survive. She had no idea; and the warthogs sat silent for a while thinking about it.

There was a full moon. The termite mounds cast long shadows on the silvery ground. Sheena could see all of the other five burrows in the circle of which hers was a part. Five sets of tusks gleamed in the moonlight.

For the first time Sheena had a sense of how leisurely existence in the bush could be. She'd been much too busy so far to appreciate that. Wildlife videos always gave the impression that life in the game parks was one mad chase and chomp, that animals were constantly being killed, left, right and middle.

It wasn't really like that. If you weren't actually hunting or being hunted – and that was true most of the time for most animals and all of the time for some – then all you had to do was *be*. That was an important freedom.

'And what next?'

The warthogs had done enough thinking about the young giraffe. Sheena began again.

As the story continued her listeners started to grind their teeth together. That was a bit off-putting; but at least they weren't using their canines to get her to talk, like the baboons had done.

She complained about the noise.

'We're just sharpening our lower tusks against our big ones.'

'The big ones do the frightening.'

'But it's the lower ones that do the fighting.'

'We keep them very sharp.'

'Sorry.'

'We'll stop.'

'Carry on.'

'Please.'

By the time she finished telling her tale she was very tired. Her final sentence had been extremely long, and in it she had given the warthogs all sorts of reasons why they should help her find the lions.

When she got to the end of the sentence there was silence. The next round of comments just didn't start. Then the first warthog snored, then the second, then the third, and so on until it was Sheena's turn. She did what was expected of her.

Chapter Ten: Simba

There was a sudden clatter and drumming of hooves and Sheena opened her eyes into the early sunlight just in time to see all five warthogs burst out from their burrows at high speed, like tubby steam trains out of dark tunnels. Since the tunnels were facing inwards in a circle the warthogs nearly crashed into each other and had to swerve sharply. Then they all raced off across the open ground, in different directions.

'What's happening? Are we being attacked? Have the lions come?' she called out after them.

'No, no, nothing like that. That's how we always start the day.'

This was from the warthog who trotted back first, much more slowly than he'd left. They hadn't gone very far. To Sheena it had seemed as if they had been dreaming about running very fast and their little legs had suddenly caught up with their big dreams and propelled them out into the morning.

'We're never absolutely certain that nothing has crept close during the night and is lying in wait for us, you see. If there was something nasty there we'd just keep on running.'

Sheena preferred a more leisurely start to her day. She crawled out of the hole now and stretched. She had slept better than she had done since she had lost the Allens.

She was hungry, and went off to the foot of the tree to see if she could surprise something edible among its roots. She didn't much mind what, as long as it was meaty: she'd decided she was

Carnivarious.

She'd have moved away in any case, since the warthogs were lining up again.

When she came back she was less hungry. There had been a fat agama lizard sitting on a rock near the tree, enjoying the sunshine. Now there was only a purple and green tail, twitching in the rock's shadow.

'Lazy lackadaisical lizards are liable to get licked up and swallowed whole,' Sheena said to herself as she returned to the termite mounds.

'Time for breakfast,' said one of the warthogs.

'Had it thanks,' said Sheena.

'What?'

'Lizard.'

'Poor little thing.'

'We've all got to eat,' said Sheena.

'No. I meant poor little thing *you*, having to make do with clammy food like that.'

'Well, wet grass is clammy.'

The other warthogs had gone off to feed underneath the tree, where the short grass had dew on it.

'I only eat grass when I need to clean out my stomach,' Sheena continued. 'It makes me bring everything up.'

'Well if I wanted to make myself puke *I'd* eat a slimy *lizard*,' said the warthog.

'Just shows – we're all different,' said Sheena.

She was beginning to realise that more and more.

When the warthogs had finished eating, they came back to the termite mounds. Sheena was sitting in the shade of the one she'd slept under.

'We've decided to help you.'

They had been grunting as they ate, not talking; so they must have talked instead of grunting when they were lined up earlier. Had they heard some of her reasons last night after all, as they were falling asleep?

'We've decided to help you find the lions – but please excuse us if we don't get too close to them.'

'How close is too close?'

'Oh, about a mile. They're very hungry these days.'

'If you take me to where I can see them that's all I need.'

They set off straight away. That pleased Sheena; and the warthogs kept their poop stops down to a minimum – only two further ones during the rest of the morning. She hoped that wasn't difficult for them.

They did pause on one other occasion, at a muddy hollow. There was nothing in it that they could have drunk, but the warthogs rolled in the malodorous black slime; then they rolled in it some more, and by the time they had finished they were covered in it from tusk to tail.

'Needed that. We have no sweat glands to help us keep our temperature down, so a coating of mud keeps the sun off…and it gets rid of bugs. Hope you didn't pick up any of those in the burrow last night.'

Sheena hadn't felt any bug bites, and she wasn't too hot, so she just watched while the warthogs dried from black to grey before setting off again.

When the sun was well past its highest point in the sky they stopped once more.

'That's it.'

'As far as we go.'

'Lions are over there.'

'How do you know?'

(There were no lions in sight.)

'Smellem.'

Sheena sniffed but could smell nothing.

'Hearem.'

She could hear nothing either. If the lions were indeed a mile away, this was impressive. But then the warthogs were altogether impressive animals.

'Noseeyem,' Sheena said.

She remembered noseeyems from her earlier life in the Caribbean. They were tiny flies, like mosquitoes, and you didn't know they were there until they bit you. She hoped the same wouldn't be true of the lions.

'Gofindem,' said one of the warthogs.

'Bye,' said a second.

'Bye.'

'Bye.'

'Bye.'

There was no doubt that she was being told she was on her own now.

'Goodbye, and thank you *very* much.'

She set off. She passed a patch of scrub and found herself heading towards some large acacias in the distance. She would soon lose sight of the warthogs. She looked back. They were standing in a line, and she thought she could hear some happy grunting.

She had no idea what she would do when she got to the lions. Strolling up to them and starting a conversation would be very risky. Either they'd be hungry, and she wouldn't get to the end of her first sentence ('I wonder whether you'd mind telling me oo er' crunch slobber slobber); or they wouldn't be, in which case they might let her get to the end of the sentence and then realise she was a spy ('I wonder whether you'd mind telling me why you've started to eat baboons oo er' crunch slobber slobber).

It would be better if she could sneak up on them and listen in to their conversation. There was no guaranteeing however that they would say anything 'useful', at least in time for her to take it back to the baboons and get the information she wanted in exchange; and she even began to wonder whether these would *be* the lions that were causing all the trouble.

She had passed through the acacias and was now crossing open grassland, trying as far as possible to stay among the taller clumps so that she couldn't be seen by anything that might be watching – she was aware that lions might well not be the only dangerous animals around. There was a single tree some way ahead, and beneath it, in the black shadow it created, were several sand-coloured lumps. They were very still, and even with her keen eyesight she couldn't be sure they weren't just boulders.

She slowed right down until she was moving one paw at a time.

Then one of the boulders rolled over and stuck its legs in the air, and she knew she had found the lion pride.

There was nothing but open ground between her and the tree. So much for sneaking. Lions had eyesight just as sharp as hers, and were particularly good at detecting movement, so she didn't dare take another step forward. Going back and around wouldn't help either – the ground was equally open on the other side of the tree. There was no way of getting close.

So she settled down where she was. Something else would have to happen before she could do more. In the meanwhile she could only watch.

There was nothing *to* watch, however. The legs stayed in the air for a long time. Then an ear twitched. And that was it.

Sheena did begin to distinguish one lion from another amid the tangle of bodies. She decided their name should be spelt 'lie-ons'. Four were lying motionless on the grass; one was draped over a fallen tree trunk; and at least three more (she couldn't be sure how many) were lying on top of each other in a twisted pile as if they were made of toffee and had melted together in the heat.

The heat got to Sheena as well after a while. The clump of grass behind which she was trying to stay hidden didn't offer any shade, and by now the air was shimmering under the burning sun so that the grass further off towards the lions seemed to shift and waver, even though there was not the slightest wind.

There was nothing else for it. Sheena went into one of her trances.

When she came out of it the sun was not so high in the sky. Another valuable day was slipping by.

While she had been in the trance she had as usual stayed distantly aware of what was happening around her…which didn't matter very much, since nothing had been. Occasionally a lion had got up and walked around the tree then settled down again with a slow, heavy flop. Several had, at different times, rolled over onto their backs for a while. One lion had stood up, stretched, and then strolled off into the distance and become lost in the heat haze.

'If the lion's the King of the Beasts then his throne should be a bed and he should have a nightcap as a crown,' Sheena thought. 'Lions may be known for their roar but they should really be famous for their snore.'

She had realised though that these lions were females —

Simba

lionesses (but 'lions' will do for short). Females always formed the core of a pride. The males would be off somewhere else, either patrolling their territory or, as seemed much more likely, fast asleep under a different tree.

Then things began to happen – but not on a large scale, rather on a small one.

Not all of the brown shapes were lions. There were some real boulders beyond the tree, and a low termite mound; then there was the tree trunk on which one of the lions had spread herself. Among all of that there must be a cave or hollow, for suddenly three lion cubs, small, striped and fluffy versions of the other lions, came tumbling out into the open and began to cause mayhem among the dozing group. There was no knowing what the cubs had been doing all afternoon: maybe the lions had had the good sense to put them in the cave and block the entrance with a rock.

If so they were going to pay for that now. The cubs began fighting and rolling in the dust, snarling at and jumping onto, into and over each other. Then they turned their attention to the dozing lions. They pulled tails with their claws, bit ears with teeth which Sheena imagined would be very sharp, climbed up onto stomachs and slid down the other side, and jumped on heads. The only response they got was an occasional indulgent lick.

Sheena disapproved. She had never had kittens herself and saw all of this as an attack on adult dignity. If she'd been there instead of here behind this clump of grass she'd have taken those young rapscallions in hand and taught them some respect for their elders. The fact that they were as big as she was wouldn't have stopped her; but the fact that their parents were twenty times as big kept her where she was.

That and the fact that a part of her was enjoying the sight.

There was something very *warm* about it all. Sheena knew deep down that she would have liked to have kittens, even if it had sometimes meant being jumped on and having her ears chewed by teeth like needles. Yes, she had Thomas and Amy, and she felt protective towards them; but they were sort of second best; and she wondered now, as she watched the cubs tire of their game and lie down, one of them nestling into a female to feed, just what that would have felt like, to have a small pink mouth taking her milk. She would never know.

Second best or not, she loved Thomas and Amy and wanted to be with them. So she had to find a way of moving things along.

Then something happened on what for her was nearly a much bigger scale, since she came close to being eaten.

She had been intent on watching the cubs at play and was therefore taken wholly by surprise by a movement to one side of her. She turned her head slightly and saw, no more than a few metres beyond her clump of grass, a very large lion with a black mane. The mane was like a broad, spade-shaped beard around the lion's face and down the front of its chest. This was not another female, but a great male.

He was walking slowly forward, but not directly towards her, and not towards the pride either. He clearly had things on his mind, and he hadn't seen her. Luckily she had been so lost in her own thoughts about what she might have missed by not being a mother that she hadn't moved a muscle for several minutes.

'He must be a pretty dopey lion,' the part of her brain which wasn't plain frightened thought. 'I *am* black-and-white, after all.'

The rest of her brain was plain *very* frightened. If he saw her and came towards her she could only run; and when something runs away from a cat, large or small, it's as if a button has been

116

pressed in the cat's head and it gives chase automatically. Two bounds from a cat that big and Sheena would be in his jaws.

He still didn't see her. He walked off at an angle then stopped at a low shrub, turned his back on it and sprayed. Tom cats of Sheena's acquaintance did the same thing. It was a bit like peeing, a way of marking territory and warning other males away.

Sheena could smell the spray from where she was – a very tom-catty smell, musky and pungent, attractive and repulsive at the same time.

Then he continued walking. As he did so, and her fear subsided, Sheena noticed things about him. He was very yellow in colour for one. He was also very scrawny – big, yes, as far as length and height were concerned, but *thin*. She could see his ribs through his skin. And his fur was dry and brittle-looking. He was not at all the picture of health and strength she had expected a lion to be. That might be why he hadn't noticed her: was he sick?

He walked closer to the pride (but still not straight at them) and some of the females sat up suspiciously as if they didn't trust him. Relationships between male and female lions are shifting things, and only the males who have won (usually by fighting for it) the temporary right to a territory can approach the females who live there. Male lions will kill and even eat cubs who have been fathered by males outside their own group...which is a good reason for mothers to be suspicious.

It did seem though that this lion must be one of those who for the moment had rights over the females, for the ones who had sat up settled down again, and the male continued on his way, stopping to drink at a muddy pool off to the left and then, further on, to spray once more.

After another long while, the female who had wandered off earlier came back.

The other lions knew she was coming, it seemed, before they could see her. Some of them had stirred. Two had stood up and looked in the direction she had taken. Then she appeared, walking towards them at the same slow pace as when she left.

All the lions except the nursing mother stood up; then the cub who was sucking had to let go as she too got to her feet.

Now Sheena realised that all the lions, not just the male who had passed by, were scrawny-looking. They couldn't all be sick, so they must be hungry. Even an animal with a reputation as fearsome as that of the lion could go short of food.

Much greeting now went on, much deep purring, licking of faces and rubbing of shoulders, and not only between the returning lion and the rest: they all seemed to be greeting each other as if the whole pride had been separated for a long time.

Even the vexatious cubs were included.

'All very well this kissy kissy,' snorted Sheena, 'but what do they do when they've really been apart?'

The answer was that they were never really apart. They lived together, slept together, hunted together and fed together. The mothers nursed each others' cubs, and cubs from different mothers often shared the same father. This was as 'apart' as they got, when one or more of the pride went off to find out where the food was.

Sheena had never experienced anything like this kind of communal living. Few other cats had. Lions are the only fully social members of the cat family (although cheetahs spend some time in twos and threes): other kinds of cat lead solitary lives.

Sheena would have argued that 'solitary' isn't the same as 'lonely', and that in any case cats have friends, like Toby. But only lions co-operate to make life easier and safer for each other.

All the adults were now facing in the direction from which the single female had returned. The cubs had disappeared into their hole as if they knew what was expected of them. Then the lions started walking.

They set off towards a part of the landscape where the grass was longer, and eventually disappeared into it. They had gone on a hunt, Sheena decided. All that licking and rubbing had been a set of signals: they had been preparing for a joint enterprise.

For a moment Sheena was tempted, stupidly, to follow them. She'd come North to do some chasing, hadn't she? Here was an opportunity to go chasing with the big girls.

But she remembered what Kenge had said: 'Thingss that chasse...', and she knew very well that if she went off recklessly into that long grass without knowing what she was doing she might well find herself on the pointed end of a hunt, if not by the lions then by something equally toothy.

In any case running round the countryside wouldn't take her any closer to the Land Rover and the Allens.

Instead she should be working on her career as a spy. She had some ideas about that.

Chapter Eleven: Simba Tena

The lions would return to the acacia tree sooner or later, fed or unfed: the cubs were still there. This was Sheena's chance to get closer to where they would probably lie down once more and perhaps say useful things.

She needed to be up in the tree by the time they came back. But they might see her up there, and would certainly smell her.

Then she remembered the warthogs and their mud bath. She walked over to the pool the male lion had drunk from. There was hardly any water in it, but the black mud around the edges was sloppy and gleaming.

Sheena, the cleanest of cats (which are very Clean) lay down in the mud – colder than she had expected – and rolled around. She twisted on her back in the wet sludge, squirmed on her sides in it, squelched her stomach down into it, dragged her stumpy tail through it, stuck her face in it, and when she eventually stood up she felt very heavy and very dirty. She also felt wonderfully free, as if she'd broken all sorts of unnecessary rules. She wished Toby could have seen her like this: she'd often wanted to surprise him, just because he was the kind of cat you could never surprise.

She felt very *secret* too, which was a good thing for a spy to be.

Although there wasn't nearly enough water in the pool for her to see her reflection, she felt satisfied with her appearance, which she thought must be like that of a sewer rat who'd lost his footing and fallen in the goo. She wasn't so sure, however, that she had fully covered up her house-cat smell: this mud wasn't as sulphurous as the last lot had been.

She had a solution. She walked over to where the male lion had sprayed. Some of the liquid he had squirted over the bush was still dripping yellowly from its leaves. Its smell was overpowering and made her feel light-headed for a moment. All she had to do was rub her slimy body against the wet leaves and she became one of those mixed creatures she'd met recently: she was a cat who looked like a muddy rat and smelt like a lion.

Now all she had to do was climb the tree and wait.

The first part of that might not be so easy. She realised that the mud was already beginning to dry on her and turn grey: it was late afternoon but there was still a lot of heat in the sun. In no time she was hard on the outside and could walk only stiffly, rocking from side to side as if she was once more copying Twiga.

This worried her a bit. She'd seen Mum Allen using a sort of mud pack on her legs to remove the hair. Would this mud, when it set really solid, take her fur off with it when it eventually fell away? She didn't want to end up bald. *'In inclement climates coatless cats constantly catch cold,'* she thought to herself.

That, though, was a difficulty for another day. She rocked slowly over towards the tree and then around it, looking for the best way up.

When she got back to where she had started, the spot where the lions had been lying, she saw three round little faces peering at her from underneath the tree trunk. The lion cubs had poked their heads out of the hole they were supposed to be hiding in. They'd probably heard Sheena clanking over towards them like a horse in armour.

The heads shot back into the hole. Sheena hoped it was because she looked awesome, but suspected it was because she looked awful.

Here was another problem, then, a much more immediate one than possible baldness. The cubs would give the game away when the rest of the pride came back. She had to do something to make sure that didn't happen.

'Hello!' she said in one of her sweeter voices (cats have lots of voices).

Only some whiskers and a nose appeared, briefly, and they were immediately pulled back into the hole.

'Hello! I'd like to talk to you.'

'Go away. We aren't allowed to talk to *you*.'

The voice was slightly squeaky, but that might be because the cub was frightened. The trio had obviously been warned to have nothing to do with strangers, no matter how sweetly they spoke.

Then suddenly a furry, sand-coloured body burst out of the darkness of the hole and landed with a thud in front of Sheena, growling in a voice as deep as it could manage. It jumped up onto the large rock above the hole so that it was looking down on Sheena. It snarled, and Sheena was impressed.

This was clearly a male cub who had decided to show how male he was (even though he was only a mini-male, more like a toy lion from the shelf in Amy's bedroom, above Annie's special chair). His bright eyes were glaring and his little claws were digging into the surface of the rock as if he was about to spring.

'You heard what my sister said: go away or you'll get trouble.'

'Yes. Go away!'

His sister had come out of the hole, but she stayed down at ground level. She wasn't quite as chunky as her brother.

'Yes. Go away!'

This echo came from the squeakiest voice of all so far. The third cub, who now came out hesitantly from the hole, was smaller than the other two, and his head looked a bit wobbly.

Sheena hadn't noticed any of those differences among the three of them when she'd watched them play from a distance: they'd had a rare old time together.

'Certainly!' Sheena said, and she turned awkwardly and started to walk away.

With her cat's sixth sense, however, she knew what was happening behind her. The cubs were looking at each other with a mixture of surprise, relief and disappointment. You can work out for yourself why they were feeling all three of those things at the same time.

The surprise lasted only a moment, however; and as she moved further away the relief got weaker and the disappointment stronger.

'Wait! Before you go tell us who you are.'

Sheena thought quickly. She had to give them a name which would reassure them. They would never believe she was a cat. There were no rats in the Park as far as she knew – and rats were not to be trusted anyway.

'Pangolin. I'm a pangolin.'

She remembered what pangolins looked like – rather like *her* in her present state, with a pointed front end and a round body covered in grey armour plating. Their tails were larger than hers, but then most tails were. Pangolins ate ants and termites and so were no threat to lion cubs.

'So why do you smell like a lion?'

'Well, I was under a bush over there and one of you came and sprayed all over me. Yuk.' (She was careful not to make the 'yuk' too emphatic: there was more than one kind of lion pride.)

'Where are you going?'

'Up this tree.'

Sheena had no chance of climbing the acacia without the cubs knowing, so she might as well come clean – in one sense.

'I've had termites for lunch and I fancy some tree ants as dessert. They're sweeter than termites because they take sugar from the tree sap.'

She was making this up as she went along and was rather impressed by herself. She could only hope that all this menu chat would allow the cubs to see her as a harmless oddity and lose interest in her. The real question was whether or not they would say anything to the other lions, when they returned, about this strange, stiffly-moving creature that had gone up into the tree above their heads.

'Bye.'

There was nothing more Sheena could do down here to make

things safe for herself, so she turned to the tree in order to climb it.

She tried what should have been an easy jump onto the lowest branch. But she hadn't reckoned with her increased weight and the fact that her back legs were encased in what was almost concrete. She fell short of the branch, clattered into the trunk of the tree and crashed to the ground.

The lion cubs had been watching closely and now burst out laughing. Sheena tried to make the best of it.

'This doesn't come easily to me, you know. I'm a ground pangolin not a tree pangolin.'

'You should stay on the ground then,' said the bold little male cub.

'You'd better,' his sister added. 'You're coming to bits.'

Sheena turned her head – with difficulty – and saw that a large lump of caked mud had fallen off her side, revealing some white fur *and* some black fur underneath.

'Oh dear,' she said, 'I'm shedding. What a nuisance. It's because of a sugar deficiency in my diet. That's why I need the tree ants.'

She jumped up towards the branch again, this time with more success.

'Don't you want the bit that fell off?' the smallest cub squeaked up after her. 'You'll be able to lick it when your tongue's sugary and stick it back on.'

'No, it's ok thanks: I'll grow some more scales soon.'

Sheena hoped all of that had sounded convincing, and that the cubs would be so excited when the lions brought food back that they wouldn't think of mentioning her.

She was wrong about the excitement, because she was wrong about the food. There was none.

She had climbed high enough into the tree for her blurred grey shape to be difficult to see from the ground below. She had lost sight of the lion cubs and hoped they had gone back into the hole where they were supposed to be. The more normal things looked when the lions returned, the better.

She waited, uncomfortably, her hard muddy shell making it difficult to bend her body to the shape of the branch she was lying along. She was afraid she'd break in the middle.

Eventually she heard the pride come back, heard them grumbling even before they reached the tree (she had carefully risked cracking in order to scratch some of the mud out of her ears, so that she would miss nothing). The voices were deep and soft, with a troubled rumble in them.

'No meat again. It's a good job you found those ostrich eggs. We'll have to move on.'

'It'll be no better anywhere else. The grazers will have gone down to the Mbanganero Swamps, and there are too many lions down there already; or they'll be up beyond Sembene, and that's too close to the cattle areas for us. You know what those herdsmen are like about their cows.

'No, things won't get any better until the rains arrive and the grazers come back here.'

Sheena guessed the grazers would be wildebeest and impala and zebra and such like. No wonder she hadn't seen many animals so far: most of them had gone where there was more water.

By now the lions had reached the tree and were beginning to settle themselves. Sheena could see something of what was happening down below. The cubs had come tumbling noisily out of the hole, but their excitement at seeing the grown-ups again was soon swamped by the gloominess of the returned hunters.

Not much licking had gone on, and the lions were in no mood to listen to the cubs – which was just as well as far as Sheena was concerned, for the cubs couldn't hold back their news.

'A pango-lin came while you were away.'

'Bits fell off him.'

'He said he was going up into the tree to look for ants.'

'To stick his bits back on.' The smallest cub had to have his say. He thought his idea had been a good one.

'There's one of the bits over there, at the foot of the tree.'

An adult lion walked over and sniffed the lump of dried mud that had fallen off Sheena's side.

That's not pangolin smell, that's male smell. Has that yellow fellow been around again?'

'Maybe. The pango-lin said it got sprayed on by a lion.'

'And it's still up in the tree.'

But the lions had no interest in pangolins. Pangolins rolled themselves into a tight ball when they were attacked, and had sharp-edged scales that could easily slice a lion's paw open if it tried to prise them apart. Pangolins were not lion food, even in hard times like these. In any case there was grown-up talk to continue, and that was more important than anything cubs might have to say.

'I'm beginning to see why Nyanya has started to eat baboons.'

Sheena had been holding her breath while the cubs tried to get the lions interested in her. Now that the topic had changed she could breathe out.

When she did so, however, another lump of mud cracked, fell off, and skittered down through the tree branches. Just when the conversation was taking an interesting turn. The lions paused, listening; but then they continued.

'Maybe; but you won't catch *me* eating them. Their meat tastes bad even when it's fresh. Besides, they're a real handful in a group. A lion in Masambo got eaten by baboons himself, once. They caught him up a tree where he had no business to be. Those Masambo lions! Those baboon teeth!'

'But you can't blame Nyanya. We don't let her share our food any more, even when we have some. And she's too old and lame now to do any real hunting herself.'

'Of course we don't feed her. That's the rule. Menfolk first (even when *we've* done the catching), then us, then the cubs *if* there's any food left, then the old and sick lions – if they can manage to gnaw the scraps before the vultures get their greedy beaks to work.

'Nyanya's had a good life. She was a good mother; and some of us are descended from her. But her time has come. It doesn't make sense to use precious food keeping her alive when she's no use to anyone any more, not even to herself. The hyenas would do us all a favour if they took her.'

Sheena didn't like this talk. She wasn't all that young herself, and the thought that the Allens might stop feeding her because her 'time' had come was rather upsetting. She'd never thought, either, that the point of living was to be of use. It was life itself which had to be used, to enjoy yourself with. Sucks to 'making sense'! That sounded like the subject Dad Allen taught – Economics. Sucks to Economics too, then!

'She was behind us on the way back – did you see her? She must have been hoping that we'd caught something and were carrying bits of it back for the cubs. She'll be here soon, you'll see.'

Indeed she was.

A lion walked in past the fallen tree and stopped. She had appeared suddenly, as if she'd emerged from the hot, dusty earth.

She waited as if she was hoping to be greeted. None of the other lions got up, however.

Sheena guessed 'Nyanya' meant 'The Old One'. Everything about her sagged. Her notched ears and her dull yellow eyes drooped, and her yellow teeth leaned at different angles. Flaps of skin hung loosely beneath her neck. Her stomach was like an empty canvas postbag that swung beneath her as she walked and pulled tight the thin flesh over her ribs. If she had been lying down on her side she would have looked like an ancient, recently-discovered skeleton waiting for an archaeologist to brush off its light covering of sand. It was as if she was slowly sinking down towards the ground and would soon collapse onto it, never to rise again. Her scarred and scabbed coat had the same dry, dusty appearance as the hard sand on which she stood, and it seemed that when she did finally fall she would simply disappear.

She walked into the shade of the largest of the rocks and lay down, slowly and stiffly.

She was the most terrible thing Sheena had seen in the Park.

When the old lion spoke, though, Sheena could hear a sharpness in her voice, weak though it was, and she imagined there would be a spark at the back of those dim eyes.

'So, no food again, eh?'

Nyanya sounded to be gloating, creakily, as if a prophecy she had made had come true.

'No food.'

'What next, then?'

'We wait.'

'Wait? I've had enough of waiting. I've had enough of waiting for you to catch some food, and give me some. I've had enough of waiting to die. So I've been doing some catching of my own.'

'We heard. But when the baboons catch *you*, you'll wish you'd been a bit more patient, and a bit more choosy about your food.'

It didn't seem to matter which individual lion was replying to Nyanya: what Sheena heard was a group voice.

'Patient is it? When you've only got weeks, or days, left there's no time for patience. Choosy is it? I'd choose to go down under a pile of baboons any day, rather than be crushed to death by unkindness!'

Here was fighting back indeed. Words could stay sharp even when teeth and claws had become blunt. Sheena could only admire.

'Baboons don't taste so bad anyway, particularly baboon babies: their skulls are quite crunchy, and juicy inside. And there are things other than baboons to catch without chasing all the way down to the swamps.'

The lions were paying more attention now. News of food was always worth attending to, and she had made their mouths water by talking about juiciness and licking her lips.

'I was over at the Far River yesterday. There are people there, in those tent things. They don't have a game scout with them, and there's no smell of guns. I'm going back when I'm hungry enough. And I'm hungry enough now.'

Sheena nearly called out, 'What colour tents? Is there a Land Rover?' for she had suddenly become afraid.

'You? You by yourself? People are twice as big as baboons and you're only half as strong as a lion should be. Even without guns they'd be too much for you.'

'Come with me then.'

'No, no! Do you know how much trouble that would bring us? We'd be labelled man-eaters and they'd hunt us down and shoot us. You'd better stay away from people, for all our sakes.'

'Death is so close that I don't much care if it comes the last little way by teeth or by bullets. I just don't want it to come by starvation. I've been hungry long enough, and I've felt better since I ate those baboons than I have for a long time. You're all too proud, that's your trouble, and too used to an easy life; and you lack courage.

'As far as being strong enough is concerned – well, children aren't much bigger than baboons and they don't have sharp teeth, or claws. There are two of them there…and they sleep in a tent by themselves.'

'Oh! Oh!' Sheena cried out inside, and she very nearly shouted it out loud as well. That couldn't be! The lions couldn't be allowed to attack Thomas and Amy! No!

She almost leapt down and went for the old lion there and then. She might be able to inflict some damage before the pride recovered from the sight of a lump of mud hurtling down onto Nyanya from the tree above. Her little teeth wouldn't do much harm, but her claws might – a blind lion wouldn't be able to hunt.

But if she failed...

She must deal with this in another way, must stay alive to deal with it, must think of a plan.

The safest thing would be to stay close to Nyanya and follow her when she left. When they were close to the family's campsite Sheena could run on ahead and do something. Exactly what, she had no idea; but this was the only way to find and warn the Allens without returning to the baboons first. That would take much too long and was too uncertain.

Nyanya was already on the move.

'I'll be back in a day or two; and my stomach will be fuller than yours.'

She walked slowly off, limping and looking harmless; but that parting comment terrified Sheena. She must follow!

She just had to hope that the lions would be watching Nyanya's departure: she had no time to check. She half slid, half scrambled and then finally jumped down from the tree on the side away from the pride. Bits of cracked mud flew off her as she began to run, firstly away from the lions, then in a wide circle that would allow her to catch up with Nyanya. She couldn't worry about camouflage now. Speed was more important. Even a limping lion could, over time, outdistance a little cat.

Chapter Twelve: Nyanya

Sheena would have liked to be able to run a bit, hide a bit to make sure she was safe, walk a bit, then run some more; but she knew she had to keep going until she caught sight of Nyanya, even if that meant heading out over open ground without stopping first to check that there was nothing fierce walking around up ahead. If there was something fierce *lying* around up ahead she was likely to make things easy for it by running straight towards it.

Nyanya must have made some kind of detour. When after a while Sheena paused and looked round, she was shocked to see the old lion coming along behind, in the distance. She hid in the grass until Nyanya trudged by.

Nyanya herself didn't seem to be worried about things jumping on her. She was now limping in a straight line and making no attempt to avoid shady spots where other animals might be hiding.

Of course she was a lion; but she was an old and tired lion, and hyenas in particular might fancy their chances against her. They wouldn't be put off by her thin, worn look: no matter how tough her flesh might be, their powerful jaws would allow them to rip her apart, and they would then be able to crunch her bones down to fine splinters and swallow them. The warthogs had pointed some hyena droppings out to Sheena, and explained why they were white.

'Bone dust,' they had said.

'Calcium,' Sheena had thought. She'd watched chemistry homework being done as well.

Now she was thinking about Nyanya, as she began to follow her, running from one clump of grass to another and hoping that the lion would not turn round suddenly and see her. She was far enough back for the little pounding sound her paws made not to matter; and since there was no wind to carry her scent forward, it also didn't matter if by now her inner domesticat smell was leaking through her outer, male lion stench.

Yes, it would solve Sheena's problem in one way if something ate Nyanya before she got anywhere near Thomas and Amy, and she even began to think up a madcap plan to find some nearby hyenas and get them to chase her back to where Nyanya was. Or maybe she could get Nyanya to chase *her*, and lead the lion into a trap.

136

Nyanya

But she couldn't go looking for hyenas without losing Nyanya; and Nyanya was her only link with the family. So arranging to have the old lion crunched up wasn't such a good idea anyway. She'd then have no way of finding the Land Rover without going all the way back to the baboons and trying to convince them that she was a little heroine who had saved the troop from further attack by a ferocious (that's how she would have put it) baboon-eater.

Besides, her feelings about Nyanya were rather confused.

She was horrified at the thought of Nyanya's claws ripping through the little green tent and those jaws (even if their teeth were worn and crooked) fastening themselves around Amy's leg and dragging her out into the open and off into the bush to be eaten at leisure. But she had also realised that Nyanya had a desperate desire to live out the last short stretch of her life as well as she could...and she had a right to do that.

Sheena had to get in the way, that was all, had to ensure that the Allens were warned or that Nyanya was somehow frightened off. The old lion could then carry on living as best she could (Sheena wouldn't mind too much if that meant eating more baboons) and the Allens could drive home safely, with a little cat tucked away in the back of the Land Rover. And when they got back to their house...

But Sheena was leaping ahead too quickly, in her imagination, to a happy ending, and that would only come if she found a way.

She was having to zig-zag a lot to stay behind the small amount of cover provided by the grass, which was short here. Luckily Nyanya had slowed down, and twice Sheena hung back behind a clump of trees to let the distance between them increase. She had to take care, however, not to lose sight of her altogether. It was now dusk, and she imagined the lion would

137

before long stop for the night: it hadn't sounded as if she was planning to go directly back to the tents.

Night, as usual, fell quickly, and the light browns and greens of the vegetation became an indistinct bluey grey as the sun sank from the sky. Nyanya stopped to drink at another almost-dried-up pool, then turned aside to a solitary acacia and lay down under it.

There were a lot of large trees not too far away, the beginnings of what seemed to be an extensive stretch of woodland. Sheena chose one that looked climbable for her but not for larger creatures, and went up it as quietly as she could. Much of the mud had fallen off her while she was running after Nyanya, so she had no trouble in reaching a fork high up in the tree from which she could see Nyanya's dark shape under the acacia. The noises of the day had stilled and the night-noise had not yet begun.

She settled down to rest.

Chapter Thirteen: Chatu

Sheena did not sleep. There was too much at stake. She did not know for certain that Nyanya wouldn't leave the acacia tree before morning: old animals, like old people, don't like to sleep a lot, as if that's a waste of whatever time they have left; and The Old One might prefer to wander through the later part of the night.

So she was ready when, just as the line of the plains to the East was beginning to show against a brightening sky, Nyanya got up slowly and stiffly, shook herself and walked over to the dried-up pool.

Sheena knew she too would have to drink there before they set off, even if the water wasn't much more than runny mud and she would have to suck it in through her teeth to keep the worst of the grit out of her mouth.

She had no idea how far they would be travelling that day. That was up to Nyanya. Everything was up to Nyanya…for the moment.

She moved down to ground level – with care, so as not to attract Nyanya's attention. She then peered cautiously round the tree trunk. Nyanya was still drinking. Watching her made Sheena thirsty. She crept two trees nearer to the pool.

Then, 'Crash!' something very heavy fell on her from above, flattening her to the ground and pinning her there so that she couldn't move. It felt as if she was underneath a thick tree branch. The breath had been knocked from her body and she had to gasp once, twice, three times before she could start to wriggle free.

Wriggle she did, and succeed she nearly did also, squirming out backwards from beneath the crushing weight. But, 'Crash!' again, and another branch fell on her.

'Is the tree coming down bit by bit?' she thought desperately.

She continued to struggle, and kicked out with her back legs; but then she felt herself seized by the hind quarters, just past her bob of a tail. Sharp teeth, although small, penetrated her skin through the fur. Then they took hold further along her body and her back legs too were gripped so that she could no longer kick.

There was something awful and *slow* about this bite, as though the creature that held her was in no hurry.

Her face had been forced down into the dust so that she could see out of only one eye. Part of what was on top of her lay directly in front of that eye. It didn't look like a tree branch at all. It was olive-green with brown patches outlined in yellow. And it moved, rolling and sliding past her and then partly over her so that she felt its great heaviness once more.

What with the weight pressing down on her and the grip on her back half she could barely move. She managed to twist around slightly and look down her body. Then she knew.

She was being held tight in the jaws of a massive snake.

It was a python.

Pythons live mainly in holes in the ground. but sometimes climb trees and drop down on unsuspecting animals underneath. Sheena had been unsuspecting and now she was certainly underneath – underneath the snake…and partly inside it already.

This was very different from the other encounters she had had in the Park. This was much more serious – and more painful:

although the teeth had not gone far into her flesh, she was being squeezed by the jaws. As if that wasn't bad enough she now felt herself being rolled over, and a scaly and heavy coil wrapped itself around her upper body.

She couldn't run away because she was already caught. She couldn't wriggle out of the snake's coils because she couldn't wriggle. She probably wouldn't be able to talk her way out of things either, since conversation with her captor would be difficult – she had hardly any breath in her body and the python had a cat stuffed half way into its mouth.

At least her head was up off the ground now, and she could see more clearly. Not that that helped; in fact it frightened her even more.

The head that held her in its grip was square and scaly. She was looking directly into its eyes, which were cold and gleaming. A diamond-shaped marking covered its head, with the point touching its nose (no more than two small holes in the bony snout). Sheena was terrified to see the bottom half of her body, of which she was very fond, disappearing down a throat that seemed to be stretching to receive her as she was dragged slowly into the smooth, clammy tunnel of the snake's insides by muscles she could feel working in ripples down her legs.

At the same time the coil around her chest began to tighten, and she remembered that pythons are what are called constrictors: they kill their prey not by biting them (they aren't poisonous) but by squeezing them to death. Then they squeeze them some more to crush their bones so that they're easier to swallow.

'Well, well.'

Sheena knew the voice, slightly quavering, slightly sneering. It was Nyanya's. The old lion was standing very close, muddy slime

141

still dripping from her jaws.

'So Chatu's got you. That's what comes of snooping. Don't think I didn't know you were behind me last night. But I can't imagine why you'd want to trail around after *me*. It's not as if I was going to be catching juicy impala and leaving bits lying round for you to scavenge. What did you want?'

Sheena wasn't very happy to hear Nyanya use the past tense, *did*, as if all Sheena's wanting was now over.

'Sorry, can't talk,' she gasped. Every time she breathed out, the coil around her chest tightened a little, so that when she tried to breathe in again her lungs wouldn't expand as far as they had the time before. Soon she wouldn't be able to breathe at all.

'Need help.'

Gasp.

'Sorry, can't give you any!' said Nyanya. 'You're well on your way down to Chatu's little mottled sock. And even if I could have helped you I would have been more likely to help myself *to* you: you look as if you might have been quite a tasty little snack.'

Lots of past tenses again: 'could have helped', 'might have been', and so on. Nyanya needed some grammar lessons; or lessons in how to assist relatives in distress; or lessons in how little cats don't give up easily.

'But...'

'Sorry again – got to go: I'm having some people for supper.'

At those words Sheena began struggling again, even more violently. Nyanya was getting away; and Sheena knew who 'some people' were.

The lion walked steadily off, out of Sheena's line of vision. Sheena stretched her neck to watch her go. That was a bad move, because it elongated her body slightly, and the coils tightened once more.

'Got to...get out of...this.'

Sheena gasped again. Cats might have nine lives – but how many gasps would she be allowed before she used up one of the nine?

First of all she had to stop the slide: she wanted to go NO further into the python.

She remembered an old riddle Amy had had difficulty in understanding since she'd never lived in a house with a chimney: 'What can go up a chimney down but not down a chimney up?'

She forced her back legs to straighten against the squeeze from the python's throat, and locked her joints like the spokes of an umbrella. At the same time she dug into the sides of the throat with her back claws.

Now the bottom half of her body couldn't be drawn in any further. But the top half was still being crushed, without mercy.

Then she saw two more lengths of the snake's body sliding slowly past her, in opposite directions. The one closer to her head came to a pointed end. It was the python's tail.

Sheena knew that if a python manages to wrap its tail around something solid, it can squeeze with much more force. Maybe the python was reaching out with its tail towards the trunk of the tree, and her problem was about to get even worse.

So she twisted her head sideways until she could get her mouth around the last few inches of the tail. Then she bit.

The snake writhed. What that meant as far as Sheena was concerned was that she was rolled over and over in the snake's coils until she was dizzy; and when the writhing stopped she was upside down. The coils hadn't got any tighter; but they hadn't slackened at all either.

She had managed to hold onto the tail with her teeth. She took more of it into her mouth and bit again, more deeply this time.

More writhing. Now she was the right way up, but still held tightly.

The mouthful of tail didn't stop her from talking. She found it was possible, by turning her head sideways, to speak out of the corner of her mouth. She might be about to be transferred from the Department of Espionage to the Mincery of the Interior, but she was going to give the python a problem or two of its own first.

'Hello! Hello Out There!'

(There was enough of her In to make 'Out There' quite appropriate.)

'Hello! Hiss if you can hear me!'

What with her shortage of breath and the contortions of her mouth Sheena wasn't sure she was making any intelligible sounds.

But the snake hissed. Sheena felt the rush of cold air along her sides.

'Ssssssss.'

'Ok. Now we're going to talk. Hiss once for yes and twice for no. Do you understand?'

'Ssssssss.'

'That's no good! I can't tell whether that's one hiss or two! Try one again!'

'Sssssssss.'

'Now try two. Remember your full stops and capitals.'

'Ssss. Ssss.'

There was some hope here. Sheena felt as if she was beginning to take control; and the python was doing what it was told. Maybe its tail was very tender.

'Good. So let's try a little test. Does this hurt?'

She bit hard. There were lots of loud hisses, all running into each other.

'Sorry, that confused the hissue.

'But now you know where we lie: half way into each other. That means we can hurt each other if we want.

'We can also eat each other if we want. You can swallow me and I can swallow you until we meet in the middle, eye to eye. All we'll be able to do then is roll around in the grass until we're stepped on by an elephant.'

This was all nonsense, she knew; but pythons weren't very smart – she'd heard them described as very primitive snakes – and she'd much rather this one swallowed her nonsense than swallowed *her*. So to prove her point she grabbed the tail an inch further along. She had to open her throat to do so, but as a cat she was able to do that so that she could swallow birds and mice whole.

'This is a classic tails I lose, tails you lose situation, understand?'

'Ssssssss.'

'So why don't we just both let go?'

'Can't.'

The snake's voice was very gurgly and strangled; but at least it was managing to speak.

'Why not?'

'One-way throat. Got to swallow you all the way and digest you before I can bring your bones back up.'

That was a journey, and a transformation, Sheena did not at all fancy.

'One-way throat? Turn the sign around,' she suggested.

'Can't. Got to wait for my digestive juices to do their job first.'

Then Sheena had an idea. Jamming her back legs across the python's throat had taken some of the pressure off her hind quarters. She found she could move her tail. For once she was glad it was only a stump with a furry fuzz on it. She was remembering the monitor lizard's trick with the millipede.

She began to move her tail gently as if it was a brush and she was painting the python's throat with delicate strokes. Stroke, stroke, stroke.

She felt the python's muscles begin to relax.

Stroke, stroke, stroke, stroke.

The muscles began to ripple once more, but this time up rather than down.

Stroke, stroke, stroke, stroke, stroke, stroke.

Sheena found that her whole body was being urged forward, carried out of the python's mouth until she flopped out onto the ground, slightly slimy, slightly crushed and with a few punctures in her bum, but otherwise fine.

She had no time to waste. It seemed a lifetime (and nearly had been) since Nyanya had disappeared. But with her natural cat politeness (which if you understand cats you will know is never very far away from cat unpoliteness) she felt she should formalise her farewell to the snake. She wanted to bring closure to what had been a most unpleasant experience.

'Very squeezed to meet you. Had an absolutely gripping time.'

'My pressure,' replied the python, with more wit than Sheena had expected.

And so they parted, like two animals – or people for that matter – who have met and matched each other and hope never to meet again.

Chapter Fourteen: Manyani Tena

Nyanya had gone. The Old One had turned suddenly into The Speedy One and, quickly though Sheena ran in the same direction as the night before, there was no sign of the lion.

There was no smell of her either. The old dried-up body probably gave off no scent, at least none that Sheena could pick up. Her nose was still partially disabled by her own smell, a perfume which, even if it was marketed under a French-sounding name like *Malodeur*, wouldn't sell too well.

She had lost Nyanya.

The sun was now above the horizon. The morning was under way. Amy and Thomas would be up and about – doing what? Playing by what Nyanya had called the Far River? Maybe they were having breakfast, sitting in the shade of a tree to shield themselves from the sun's early brightness. How far away were they?

She had no means of telling. What was more important, she had no idea of the way ahead. If she carried on running like this she might end up farther from where she needed to be rather than closer to it. So she had no choice. She would have to go back to the baboons, even though that might well take too long.

She turned around there and then and headed towards the trees where Chatu was probably coiled up, recovering from having his insides raked by the spokes of a very uncooperative umbrella (cats are Contrary, as Sheena had demonstrated by insisting on travelling through the python's body in a direction very contrary to the one Chatu had intended). She stopped for a drink of sorts at the muddy pool then set off again.

She decided to take a risk. After leaving the baboon resting-place at Island Campsite, she had travelled a long way down the track before reaching the baobab tree and turning left, and then even further, via the termite mounds, to where she was now. If she ran North, she should hit the Ubi River and be able to follow it back to the baboons. That could save some time.

She came to a dried-up river more quickly than she expected, and that worried her. Was it the right one? If not, she could be taken miles out of her way. She could only hope, and run.

She ran along the bank of the river where she could, since the sand in the river bed was very soft and slowed her down. All the while she tried to reassure herself that this was in fact the Ubi River. It must be, surely – she had crossed no other river bed on her way to the lions. It must be.

She was also terrified that when (if) she reached Island Campsite the baboons would not be there. They'd told her that if they did move on it would be towards the West…and that would take them further away.

She was in some pain – from the holes in her rump left by Chatu's teeth, and from the bruising of her ribs caused by Chatu's coils. *'It's so unsociable for slithery snakes to squash small mammals then slowly swallow them.'*

After several difficult hours she saw, up ahead, what she thought might just be the large group of trees in the middle of the dried-up river. Then there was an unmistakable 'Gwahoo!'

It was manyani tena – the baboons again.

Two young male baboons raced aggressively out towards her. They escorted her to a clearing not far from the main one. The whole troop was there, foraging.

The most important baboons were soon squatting around her in a circle. The rest of the troop gathered in a wider circle beyond that.

The baboon who had sent her on her mission confronted her, his great ruff of grey hair standing up menacingly and the bristles between his eyes twitching. He began by yawning. This was not going to be easy.

'Well?'

'Well-*come* you mean,' said Sheena. 'Welcome *back*. You should be pleased to see me.'

Sheena had decided that she would need to convince the baboons that she had brought more with her in the way of information than she actually had. She was trying to sell what she had gathered from the lions, after all, and there wasn't much of it.

'We'll only be *pleased to see you*, as you put it, if we're pleased with what you tell us.'

'Will you be pleased with what I tell you if what I tell you is bad news?'

That made the baboon think a bit.

'Whether or not it's bad news is none of your business. We'll be the judges of that. Just tell us. Why have lions started eating baboons?'

'It's not lions: it's *a* lion. It's a raggedy old lion who can't hunt any more. The other lions in the pride won't give her any proper food so she's having to make do with…'

'Make *do* with! Make *do* with baboons?'

Sheena hadn't chosen her words anywhere near carefully enough. The old baboon had reared up and was towering over her with his fangs bared. He was aware that the whole troop was listening so he had to do the political thing and make a big fuss

about the insult. He gave an exhibition yawn.

'...make do with other things, even baboons which are so difficult to catch because they're so clever.' Sheena hurriedly completed her sentence more diplomatically.

The old baboon dropped onto all fours again and his fangs disappeared – at least for now.

'So where is this raggedy lion? We'll chase her and kill her and that will be that.'

That was good news; but she could only answer the baboon's question vaguely.

'Well, er...I don't know, actually.'

'What do you mean you don't know, *actually*? You were sent to find out!'

'No I wasn't. I was sent to find out something useful. I found it out and now I've told you. Will you therefore please point me in the direction of the Land Rover so that I can go and save my friends?'

'Save them from what?'

Sheena hadn't meant to say so much. The baboons might well be pleased to hear that Nyanya was turning her attention to human beings. For one thing that would be much better than that she should carry on eating baboons. For another it made it quite likely that she would be shot once it was discovered that she had attacked humans. They might therefore decide not to do anything about her.

'Oh – from anything that might happen to them. You know this place – full of nasty surprises.'

'Nasty surprises like raggedy lions?'

The old baboon hadn't become leader of the troop just by being old.

'So that's where this old lion is heading,' he pondered. 'No doubt she'll make her attack as soon as night falls. Good. We'll catch her with her mouth full.'

They wouldn't wait until humans hunted her down. They wouldn't take the chance of Nyanya escaping and attacking more baboons at a later date. They were much better at hunting than people. Besides, there were things like revenge and reputation involved. Maybe a troop of baboons should be called a pride of baboons instead, Sheena thought.

But they would wait until Nyanya had attacked the children, as if Amy and Thomas were bait.

'Should I run on ahead and...er...see how things are?'

'No.'

The baboon yawned, and this time it wasn't an exhibition yawn, it was an exclamation yawn.

'No you shouldn't. No you won't. You'd warn the people because you're a *people* cat; and you might well decide to warn the lion because you're a people *cat.*'

The baboon had stepped menacingly towards her, his nostrils flaring.

'You even smell horribly like a lion (exclamation yawn).'

Malodeur was clearly a perfume that lingered.

The other big baboons now began to press in towards her, their nostrils dilating and their teeth beginning to show between their thin lips. They were obviously not going to keep their bargain with Sheena, and she for her part was not going to hang round while they did something else. So she jumped.

She jumped in her old style, 'Just like that', before anyone had any idea of what she was going to do. She jumped clear over the heads of the baboons nearest to her and landed in the space behind them, where there were small groups of the less important baboons.

One of the big baboons whirled around very quickly and took off in a mighty leap which would have brought him down on top of her. But just as he left the ground he collided with a much smaller baboon, a female, who had moved at the same time and got in his way; and both baboons fell in a twisted heap on the ground. Sheena heard a timid voice saying, 'Sorry! Sorry!' and thought she recognized it.

That collision gave her half a chance. She raced across the clearing. She did not know where she was running to: for the moment she was running only to save her little black-and-white hide.

But she was not going to escape. There were baboons to each side of her; there were baboons ahead; and the big baboons behind were already pounding after her, screaming with rage.

Her lion smell had triggered off a mad killing frenzy in the male members of the troop. She was done for.

Her mind was running even faster than her legs. Ahead of her she saw a baby baboon sitting quietly and paying no attention to what was going. She remembered about black baboon babies. As she passed it she twisted suddenly sideways and grabbed the baby with her teeth, by the back of its scrawny neck. All the baboons started screaming now.

She jumped up onto the trunk of a fallen tree and, the baby swinging from her jaws, turned to face her pursuers.

They skidded to a halt in a cloud of dust, and suddenly looked lost. Their shifty eyes did what shifty eyes do – they shifted. They shifted away from her as if the baboons didn't want to look at her any more. Some of them even started grubbing around as if they were searching for food – their way of pretending nothing much was happening so that they didn't have to do anything.

For they didn't know what *to* do. Sheena had given the 'don't want to fight no more' signal, and they had to obey it.

But how long would their obedience last?

She never found out. At that moment there was a great whooshing in the air and a beating of wide wings. She felt the skin at the back of her own neck gripped in sharp talons, and she was lifted upwards. There was a brief time when she hung dangling below whatever massive bird had grabbed her and the baboon baby hung dangling below *her*, as if this was some three-tier acrobatic act. Then she let go of the baby and was swung up and away.

The baboons were still, and silent. There was a plop as the baby hit the ground ('Has it fallen on its head?' Sheena wondered, in a detached sort of way) but not even its mother rushed forward to pick it up.

The clearing, and the baboons with their surprised, upturned faces, shrank as Sheena was carried higher. Strangely, for the moment she was not afraid. Being borne aloft (she tried to use rather grand terms to disguise the fact that she was really being yanked upwards by the scruff of her neck) was rather better than being chomped by lions, gulped rhythmically by snakes or torn apart by baboons, which were some of the other fates she'd faced in the last few days.

It was all quite soothing, in fact: she hadn't been carried like this since she was very small. When a cat picks up a kitten in its teeth, the kitten just hangs there, limply. That's because teeth in the back of your neck, if you're a kitten (and as long as they're your mother's teeth), are a signal to relax. Signals are important, as we've noticed several times.

So Sheena relaxed and tried not to think of what might be coming next. There was no signal to tell her that.

Chapter Fifteen: Kapungu

She was not being carried any higher now, but the ground beneath was slipping smoothly past as the wings above her beat out their heavy rhythm.

The trees were a long way below, and she couldn't understand why the eagle (she had to assume eagle, but it was impossible for her to twist her head upwards to look) was flying so high. She guessed she was being taken to its nest, which was presumably at the top of a tree. So they would have to drop down again to reach it, and a lot of energy would have been wasted. But she might as well enjoy the ride, and the view – and the satisfying thought of all those baboons still standing in the clearing looking upwards, with their eyes and their mouths wide open. She was a bit sorry about the baby landing on its head, though.

Then she saw that they were heading towards a hill, and that explained why they were flying at that level. The nest would be on top of a tree, and the tree would be on top of the hill.

They were.

The hill was cone-shaped and steep-sided. (Was it Ketabong Hill?) They were aiming for a large baobab near its summit; and among the tree's bare branches was a dark, twiggy shape.

With a lot of flapping and crashing among the branches she was lowered, rear paws first, into the nest. It was soft and cool inside, but Sheena had no intention of staying there. She had been waiting for the moment when the 'relax and dangle' signal would be cancelled; and she was ready to kick, scratch and bite her way out of this little situation. She had yet to meet a bird who would be anything of a match for her at close quarters.

It wasn't going to be as easy as that, though. The nest into which she had been inserted was not flat and open like a stork's. It was more rounded, and almost completely enclosed, with a hole to one side rather than in the top.

As soon as she was on all four of her paws Sheena swung round towards the hole with her claws out, ready for anything.

Anything, that is, except the size of the orange beak blocking the exit, and the fierceness of the brown eyes to either side of it. This was indeed an eagle, and a large and ferocious-looking one. Its beak had a hooked tip, black on top and very sharp. Its face was red, which made it look angry. Its head and shoulders were also black. It was a very handsome bird.

'You're a very handsome bird,' said Sheena, pulling her claws surreptitiously back in. She had quickly decided that kicking, scratching and biting just would not do. Pecking seemed to be how things were settled around here, and she was therefore at something of a disadvantage.

'Bateleur.'

The pronunciation was somewhat French.

'I beg your pardon?' said Sheena.

'Battler? I'm sure you are, judging by the size of your very splendid beak.'

'No, Bateleur. I'm a Bateleur Eagle.'

'And I'm a Battler too.'

This voice came from underneath Sheena. The soft warm floor of the nest beneath her paws moved, and she realised it was soft and warm because it was a big, fat, brown chick, which now poked its fluffy head up and looked at her indignantly.

'Would you mind getting off of me?'

'Getting *off*, not off *of*,' said the parent bateleur.

'And Bateleur: eLEUR, eLEUR.'

'Eleur, eleur to you too,' said Sheena, trying a bit of a French accent herself.

'I'm a cat.'

'No you're not, you're lunch.'

'Oh,' said Sheena in a small voice.

'Well I hope she's not as tough as those spring hares you've been bringing back: string hares I call them.'

The chick had struggled out from under Sheena and now stood up, fluffing out its feathers. It was almost as big as she was.

'You're getting too picky over your food, young man,' said the eagle.

'You're nearly of an age when you'll have to go off and find your own. Do you realise how far I sometimes have to fly in a day to put food in the nest?'

'Two hundred air miles – you've told me two hundred times.'

Then the chick turned towards Sheena.

'My real name's Kapungu,' he said.

'No it's not!' said his father.

'That's your African name. You've got a French name and you should be proud of it.'

'I think I should be proud of my African name. That's the one I want to use, anyway.'

'You'd better talk to your mother about that when she gets back. You're getting too picky about your name *and* your food.'

Sheena let this domestic squabble take its course, hoping that some advantage to her would arise out of it. Then the chick decided to show just what being 'picky' about his food meant, and picked grumpily at Sheena's rump with his hard beak, just where her Chatu punctures were.

'Ow!' said Sheena, then smiled sweetly at the chick as if it had all been an accident. The big eagle was watching carefully. But Sheena had turned her head partly away from the hole. When she smiled she took care that the chick saw her sharp teeth and the eagle didn't. That was a little signal of her own she wanted the chick to have.

'You might not have had anything at all today if I hadn't seen this thing up on top of a log, putting on some kind of show for the baboons. I think it was trying to demonstrate how strong its teeth are – it was dangling a baboon baby in them.

'We'd have had both of them, cat *and* baby, if its teeth had been as powerful as these claws of mine…'

The eagle was making a point to Sheena – perhaps he had seen her show her teeth after all. In fact he made four points altogether, one on the end of each of the four long talons he held up for her to see.

Sheena was trying to remember a poem about an eagle Thomas had had to learn off by heart (he'd complained that *no*body had to learn poems by *heart* any more: that was *really* old-fashioned). *He clasps the cat with crooked hands* – was that it? Sheena had felt well and truly clasped on her way to the tree, and the sheer size of the eagle's talons was the reason, she now saw.

And like a thunderbolt he falls. That was the poem's last line.

'How did you do that – grab me like that I mean?' she asked.

She thought she might as well find a way to get a conversation going in the hope that through it she'd find a way to get going herself.

'You seemed to just drop out of the sky!'

Throughout all of this she had not for a moment forgotten why she had gone back to the baboons, why she needed to discover where the family were camping, why she needed to get there before dark. Nyanya.

The eagle seemed willing enough to talk. Perhaps it wasn't lunch-time yet.

'We're famous flyers, we bateleurs.

'*Bateleur* means *tight-rope walker* in French, at least the old French word means that. We're balancers — we use our wings to stay level in the air, and to steer, in the same way that a tight-rope walker uses his pole. We can't steer with our tail feathers like other birds: our tails are very short.'

'There's nothing wrong with *that*,' Sheena said.

'Then the same word in modern French…'

Sheena had tapped into the eagle's pride (a pride of eagles?) about his flying skill. Flattery was once again showing itself to be more effective than assault and battery.

'…means *acrobat*. That fits as well: we can twist and turn in the air with the best of them, even the fish eagles, and they're pretty good at it.'

'But when we flew here you came in a straight line with none of that fancy stuff.'

By now Sheena knew where she wanted the conversation to go, and she was doing some steering of her own.

'Oh, that's for the birds…er…the female birds I mean.'

Here the eagle turned to the chick.

'Don't you tell your mother I used that word, when she gets home.'

The chick's eyes gleamed.

'No of course not, Dad.'

The eagle turned back to Sheena.

'When we're courting we show off our flying skills. We do a kind of ballet in the air with the female of our choice. We hope

160

we'll become her choice also; and it's very important to make sure we can air-dance well together. We mate for life, you see.'

'And have only one egg at a time. That's me!' said the chick.

Sheena had never seen an egg with feathers before, but said nothing.

'I'd really like to see you fly like that. Do you take passengers?'

'I don't think that would work. The physics would be all wrong.'

The eagle obviously took his flying very seriously.

Sheena wanted to make a little detour here.

'I'll bet you can see a lot when you're flying. Do you have good eyesight?'

'Ha! Eyesight? Best there is! We have two sharp spots in each eye instead of just one, and a million light-sensitive cells per millimeter on our retinas.'

This was all very technical: he took his eyesight seriously as well, it seemed.

'That's five times as many as humans. It's why those bird-watcher folk with their funny hats have to look at us through a pair of tunnels with glass at either end – birdnoculars I think they call them.'

'Cats have good eyesight too, you know.'

'Show me!' said the eagle. This was proving to be a bit easier than Sheena had expected.

'All right. Let me see out!'

The eagle was very unsuspecting for such a sharp-nosed creature, and stepped back from the hole in the nest. Sheena stuck her head out.

Things were immediately made difficult by the chick, who insisted on forcing himself partially out through the hole also, below Sheena. The downy feathers on top of his head were ruffled by the breeze that was blowing at the top of the hill, tickled her nose and made her sneeze.

'Aaa-choo! Oh, sorry!' she said and licked the top of the chick's head clean before the eagle could see what she'd deposited on it.

The hill was behind and below. It was casting its shadow forward: the afternoon had almost passed. The whole of the Park to the East of the hill was laid out before her, beyond the shadow. The sand-coloured ribbon of the Ubi River snaked at an angle across the landscape. She could see way beyond it into the hazy blue distance, well past where any Land Rover could have driven in one day. The family must be down there somewhere. But there was no sign of them. It was time to get help.

'I can see...an elephant.'

She had chosen something easy just to prime the eagle's pride.

She could indeed see one, her first ever, standing still in the shade of a tree near the bottom of the hill; and she wished, fleetingly, that she had time to get closer to it.

'Yes, undoubtedly an elephant. But do you see what it's got in its trunk?'

Sheena couldn't.

'I can see...a yellow bird in a tree,' Sheena said.

In truth she could see only *something* yellow, but it was either a bird or a flower.

'Ah yes. But can you see the colour of its eye?'

'I can see...'

She had raised her head slightly.

'I can see lots of baboons running very fast.'

And she could. If they were her baboons they had covered a surprising amount of ground since she had been airlifted from the clearing. They were travelling East, following the line of the river at that point. Had they imagined she had been *rescued* by the eagle and was now on her way to warn Nyanya, or the children, or by some other means get in the way of their plan? That would explain the haste with which they were now travelling.

On her way to warn the children! If only wishes were wings, or wings could be wished!

Maybe wings could be borrowed, though…but first things first.

'I can see…'

She chose something way off in front of the running baboons.

'I can see a bare tree with a top branch that's curved like an eagle's beak.'

'Yes. But can you see the ant on the end of the branch?'

This would have been tedious by now if so much had not depended on it.

'Your turn,' said Sheena.

She hoped the eagle would select something else beyond the baboons, something really difficult, something she couldn't see at all…something special to her.

'There's a white car under a tree half as far again as the one with the eagle's beak. Can you see what kind of car?' asked the eagle.

Sheena could see no sign of a car; but, 'It's a Land Rover,' she said.

She hoped it was, oh she hoped.

'Very good. But can you read the number plate?'

'It's TZL8046. Right?'

She waited anxiously for the reply. All she needed was the eagle's confirmation. She thought for a moment she wasn't going to get it.

'No, you're wrong.'

Her heart sank.

'It's TZL8045.'

Sheena knew she had remembered the right number; but she didn't mind at all that the eagle was trying to save face by correcting her. What she minded was that Thomas and Amy were down there in danger of being eaten and she was up here, miles away. It was time for the next part of her scheme.

'Well!' she said, 'You win! Amazing! If you can fly half as well as you can see, you must be wonderful at it.

'What was that you were saying about physics? I didn't quite understand that.'

The eagle cleared his throat, then launched into an explanation as if he were pushing himself off from the branch and taking to the air – rather ponderously, Sheena thought.

'Well it's all about aerodynamics – that's the science of the interaction between air and solid bodies moving through it.'

Sheena didn't need to hear all of that. She was interested only in having her own solid body move through the air, towards where she now knew Land Rover TZL8046 was.

'A passenger would provide more wind resistance and slow the flyer down.

'Now that wouldn't necessarily be a bad thing: aerial acrobatics sometimes demand that you fly as slowly as you can without stalling.

'Then there's the ballistic factor – gravitational and centrifugal forces if you like. I can see a real advantage there. I could use my passenger (Sheena noticed the 'I' and the 'my': the eagle was becoming very interested in the possibilities) as a point around which I could swing. That would allow me to make very tight turns. We'd have to fly well out from the hill, though, to get away from the air currents: they're too unpredictable here. Yes…yes.'

Much thinking was going on.

Then, 'We could try,' said the eagle.

'What about me? Why not me?'

The chick had been listening to all of this.

'No, not you, precious, not yet. Your mother would go ballistic.' (Sheena wasn't sure how the word was being used this time, but she thought it had something to do with missiles.)

'I don't know how this will work out. If things go wrong I'll just have to let go; and you aren't equipped for that.'

Sheena wasn't ready, either, to be let go of half-way to the clouds. But she was given no choice.

Her head was still out of the nest. The eagle lifted off on his broad wings and as he did so grabbed her by the back of her neck again. She was dragged out of the nest and up into the air once more. As they swung past the highest branches she had a last view of the fat chick looking up at them, wide-eyed. Then they were climbing and climbing and moving out from the hillside towards the bare tree in the far distance.

Way off to the right, and now a long way below, Sheena could see another hill, roughly the same shape as the one they had just left – perhaps *that* was Ketabong Hill.

Suddenly the eagle folded his wings and dropped. He must be getting up speed for one of his spectacular turns, Sheena thought. But he had misjudged the weight, for acrobatic purposes, of the unusual little animal he was carrying and when he braked again by spreading his wings again, opening his tail feathers and angling them downwards, the jerk on the back of Sheena's neck was almost enough to tear her out of his grasp.

'Oo...er...clasp the cat tighter!' she cried.

The eagle dropped again, not so sharply this time; and then he began a tight turn. That had Sheena swinging outwards and around as if she was going to be slung off towards the horizon – which had tipped at an alarming angle.

The eagle swooped once more, but rose again before swinging round in the opposite direction. This turn was even tighter.

By now Sheena was very dizzy.

'This is working very well,' said the eagle.

Sheena said nothing. She was torn between encouraging him on the one hand so that he would continue the flight, and on the other screaming, 'Help! Put me down!'

'I'll just try a few more turns, then we might manage a somersault,' said the eagle.

Might manage?

It was time for Sheena to do some more steering. They had lost a fair amount of height by now, and weren't so far above the

166

ground. But they hadn't flow very far towards the bare tree either.

'Somersault? Sounds like fun!'

Sheena couldn't believe she was saying that.

'But how about we get above some trees so that if you have to drop me I'll have a softer landing?'

'Fair enough.'

'The trees look much thicker and greener further on, where we saw the Land Rover.'

'Ok.'

The eagle winged steadily and in a straight line. Sheena looked down and saw, between her dangling back legs, the baboons scampering in the same direction across the open grassland. She would have liked them to look up and see her swing past over their heads: she wanted them to get where they were going quickly, and the sight of her overtaking them would have pricked them on like an acacia thorn in their rumps. But there was no sign that they'd noticed her.

After a while they flew over the dead tree with the beak-shaped branch, and on until they were above a stretch of bright green trees that looked as if they might lie along the banks of a river. But there was no sign of water, and none of a Land Rover either. Sheena would just have to take a chance that they were in the right place.

'Ready?' asked the eagle.

'Yes,' said Sheena, and closed her eyes.

The eagle dropped again. It seemed to Sheena that they fell an awful long way, with the air rushing past her ears, before the brakes were suddenly applied and she was swung around and up and over and back down again, and then round and over again.

'Splendid! Double somersault with a half-round reverse flip! Never done one of those before!' cried the eagle, mightily pleased.

'Ever done one of these before?' asked Sheena.

'It's a triple spin with a half-nelson downwards flop.'

She twisted her body and swung out sideways as far as she could. Then she hooked her back claws into the feathers underneath the eagle's left-hand wing and pulled down on it. That immediately de-stabilised him and he began to twirl in the air. With her right front claws she reached up over her head and pushed against the point where his right leg joined his body. They began to fall.

'What are you doing?' he screamed.

'Leaving!' she replied.

Cats can be very Concise.

The eagle flapped mightily with his one free wing, but that had little effect. They spiralled downwards like a seed pod spinning down from a tree, and crashed loudly into branches which gave way under them.

The eagle did not fall far. He still had his wings out and they stopped him almost immediately. He had let go of Sheena: she had broken some major flight rules and made him do something very undignified, and he wanted to be rid of her. He would have to live with the fact that he had lost his lunch. (Sheena would have lost hers long before, if she'd eaten any.)

She had let go of the eagle, also. He had served his purpose.

She smashed through the top layer of foliage then tumbled down through the ones below that and ended up, winded, on a thick branch.

She lay there until she got her breath back, and heard the eagle breaking free of his entanglement and flapping off into the sky.

'That was fun!' she said; and she only partly didn't mean it.

Now she had to find the Land Rover.

Chapter Sixteen: Nyanya Tena

The branch she had finally landed on was well down the tree, and the surrounding trees were quite close together; so she could not see very far.

She listened, but could hear only the gentle 'hoo-hoo' of a dove.

She had got this far: where should she go from here? The second worst thing she could now do would be to head off in the wrong direction. But which was the right one?

The worst thing would be to get caught by the baboons, who might not be very far away. They would have their cat and eat it, then let Nyanya eat Thomas, or Amy, or both, then wreak their vengeance on the old lion – and possibly eat her as well.

She noticed that the trees were thinner to one side of where she was, and through them she could see an open sandy space. That might well be a dry river bed. If she went to it she would be able to see a bit further in at least two directions.

She jumped down from the tree and walked through to the open space.

This would be quite a large river when there was water in it. Its course bent sharply out of sight to her left. To her right it curved more gently away, and widened. It was mostly sand, but there were some shingly patches. Several large tree trunks had washed down from further upstream (whichever way upstream was) and settled into the sand, which in places had piled up in

169

drifts. The tree trunks had been bleached by the sun to a shiny, silvery white and were like gigantic leg bones, half-buried (or half dug up).

She decided to go left along the river as far as the first bend. She stayed on the grassy bank, once she found how difficult it was to walk in the loose sand and how hot it was out there.

There were marks in the sand, lots of marks, criss-crossing the river bed – paw prints of various sizes (some of them frighteningly large), lines where something had dragged itself or been dragged, and one set of shallow depressions the size of very large dinner plates, wrinkled on the surface. She thought they must be elephant prints. Then a little further on there were some deep holes in the sand, with the same flat depressions leading to them. At the bottom of one of the holes there was a little water. Had the elephants dug down with their trunks or their great front feet, so that they could drink?

Sheena was very thirsty. She lowered the front part of her body into the hole, pushing with her front paws against the sides to make sure she didn't slide all the way in. She couldn't reach the water. It smelt very good. She needed it.

So she let go and slipped down plop into the cool depths of the hole and the even cooler shallowness of the water. She wasn't absolutely sure she would be able to get out again; but the water tasted wonderful in her parched mouth, sweet and clean and not at all like the muddy stuff she had been forced to drink recently. She drank lots. Then she drank some more. Then she struggled around in the hole, which was quite a tight fit, jumped upwards, scrabbled a bit in the loose sand, and was out in the hot sunshine once again.

When she got to the bend she cut through the bushes until she could see the next stretch of river bed. There was another bend.

She guessed there would be another one beyond that. Perhaps it was time to stop, in case she was going the wrong way.

She was fearful of stopping, however. What if Nyanya was close? If she walked just a little further she might see her. What if the children were close? What if Nyanya was already close to the children?

She started to walk again.

It was then that she thought she heard, somewhere behind her, baboon noises. Did that mean she had indeed turned in the wrong direction? Should she go back, and risk being seen by the baboons before she had found the Land Rover?

She had just rounded the next bend. Here the river bed widened and straightened and she could see a long way.

There were two unexpected dots of colour in the distant part of the river bed, just before it curved again. One dot was red and one was blue. They were moving, slowly. She knew that Thomas had a red t-shirt and Amy a blue one. She wished she had the eagle's eyesight. She started to run in a straight line which took her down onto the sand. Her paws sank in and dragged.

There was a long way to go. She reached a point where the bank stuck out a little way, and lost sight of the red and blue dots behind it. There was a bush on the bank. There was a lion under the bush and it had seen her.

It was Nyanya. There was no mistaking her. She was indeed a raggedy lion.

Nyanya looked directly at Sheena and for the first time Sheena noticed that even though her eyes were tired-looking they were also very calm.

Then she showed her raggedy teeth and said, in her raggedy voice, 'Oh, it's you! Congratulations! Not many animals get out of Chatu's clutches, and certainly not out of his mouth. Maybe you wriggled all the way down to her tail and chewed your way out. Ha! A leaky python! I'd like to watch him drink!'

Sheena was in no mood for jokiness. Things were happening much more quickly than she had thought they would. Thomas and Amy were there, Nyanya was here, the baboons were somewhere close, and it could all turn out very badly.

From what Nyanya had said to the other lions it seemed she intended to wait until nightfall, perhaps so that she could catch the children in their tent while the Allen parents were sleeping. But her plan would change if she saw the children outside and alone. They might even walk down the river bed towards her, unless they were warned.

Nyanya must not have noticed them yet (they were hidden from her by the bush), nor heard them nor smelt them. She was after all very old.

She was several things in fact – old, but also terrible, and brave, and sad…and very dangerous. Sheena's feelings about her were still in conflict; but she had to be stopped.

Sheena could think of no way to get the lion to move from where she was, in the shade of the bush. She considered provoking a chase, away from the river; but it was unlikely that Nyanya would stir her stiff bones for such a small meal when a larger and easier one was soon going to be available.

If Sheena ran towards the children to warn them, Nyanya would get there first in spite of her limp. Thomas and Amy must surely be near the Land Rover or the tents, but near can sometimes be too far.

'Have you really followed me all this way? Have you somehow found out about tonight's special? Do you want me to leave you a little child toe or two? Maybe I will…but then maybe I won't.'

There was a touch of cruelty, too, about Nyanya.

'No thank you. Maybe some other time. I've got to go now.'

'*Got to go* doesn't tell me why you *came*.'

Here Nyanya stood up to emphasise the fact that she really wanted an answer.

'I came because I was chased. There are some baboons after me.'

That wouldn't be enough to scare Nyanya away.

'I upset them by dropping one of their babies on its head and by being a cat; and they also said I was a dunzi and I smelled bad.'

She had put together as many reasons as she could think of (some of them only half-truths) in the hope that they would be more believable as a package. None of them was convincing by itself. One of them, however, caught Nyanya's attention.

'Dunzi? Who did they think you were spying for?'

'You…Lions, I mean.'

'Which lions?'

'Any lions. Lions in general. *I'm* half lion you see, and I thought that if I found out about baboons – food being so scarce and all – you might let me hunt with you.'

'You're half lion? Ha! The other half must be all imagination!'

'Whatever you started off as, you started off too small and the wrong colour, and you stopped growing too soon. Whoever saw a black-and-white lion? You're too easily noticed to be a predator. And real hunters don't let themselves get caught by pythons no matter how clever they might be at getting away afterwards. You're no lion.'

Nyanya was even better than Sheena at stringing reasons together. She was clearly rejecting this part of Sheena's story. Sheena had to try harder.

'I'm the result of a human experiment. They took bits from a lion and bits from a mouse and put them together. You've heard of a genet-cat haven't you? Well, I'm a genetic-cat, a GMF – a genetically modified feline.'

Nyanya showed no sign of being impressed by the scientific language.

'And your colour?'

'The mouse was a white one and the lion was black.'

'Black lion? No such thing. Not round here at least. Perhaps way North, I've heard, in a place called Gorandorogo.

'That's a funny little tale you're trying to tell me; and that's a funny little tail you have as well, not at all like either a lion's or a mouse's; and you've ended up as a funny little creature, no matter how.'

'I may seem funny to you, but it's not funny being me. Nobody wants me to be one of them. I tried being a mouse but the other mice kept running away from me. So I decided to be a lion.'

'You are *not* a lion. You are not any *percentage* of a lion.'

Sheena gave up on that.

'But I *am* a *spy*! I can prove it!'

'How?'

'The baboons aren't just coming here because they're chasing me. They're coming here to kill you.'

'How do you know that?'

'I overheard them. They said that you'd been eating members of their troop. They said you'd killed a mother and her baby, then one of the troop's leaders. They want to get you for that. So when they've killed me they're going to kill you; or when they've killed you they're going to kill me. Does it matter which way round?'

Sheena was doing her best to appear frightened, and it wasn't very hard. The baboons *were* coming and they *would* kill her if they caught her.

She was also doing her best to frighten Nyanya. If only the old lion would run away and hide.

'Kill me? They're welcome to try. But they've got to find me first.

'And I'm not leaving here until I've had what I came for. My mouth's watering already. Thanks for the warning, though. I'll only be here until supper time, and I'll watch out for baboons.'

Nothing had been gained. Luckily Nyanya had shown no interest in how Sheena had come to be in the Park in the first place, and had not guessed she might somehow be connected to the family she herself was planning to attack. As animals, and people, get older, some things become less relevant to them (in other words less likely to affect what remains of their lives) and they tend to ignore them; or if they're different from what they're used to, they label them 'new-fangled' and ignore them anyway.

Sheena the genetically modified feline might in Nyanya's view be new-fangled and irrelevant; but Sheena the plain little cat was going to do her best to affect the next hour or so of the old lion's life.

Then Nyanya said something which made the situation even more urgent.

'Maybe I'll bring supper forward, however, to be safe. I'll just wait for the sun to go down, then I'll go to meet my guests.'

'Bye! See you!' said Sheena.

She now knew she had to act very quickly. She'd tried to make things better by telling Nyanya about the baboons, but she'd made them worse.

Nyanya did not reply; she just lay down, slowly.

Sheena walked casually out into the river bed. Nyanya was watching her. The red and blue figures were still there in the distance, screened from Nyanya by the bush. Yes, it was Thomas and Amy, she was now sure. They were bending over, probably digging around in the shingle looking for coloured pebbles. Amy liked to collect pebbles because they were pretty. Thomas scoffed at that: he was developing an interest in geology and collected rocks so that he could find out how they had been formed millions of years ago.

Sheena was surprised their parents had let them go off on

their own like that. The Land Rover *must* be nearby.

Now Sheena had to take a chance. Several chances in fact.

She had to hope that the children would not wander any closer.

She had to trust that Nyanya would not move while the sun was in the sky.

She had to believe that the baboons were close.

Then, beyond chances, she had to take a risk.

So, without looking at Nyanya again, she turned and ran back the way she had come, back to the tree she had landed in, then beyond that. For some reason the baboons had arrived at a point South of the campsite, and South of where Kapungu had dropped her. With luck they would be loping along towards where they knew the Land Rover to be. All she had to do was find them, hurry them up, and make sure they found Nyanya.

When she did locate them she was disappointed. It was the whole troop; but they had stopped.

They were not too far from the dry river bed (she heard a bark not long after she had run past the tree, and headed in that direction). That was good: she would just have to divert them slightly. If you want to divert something, however, it first of all has to be moving. The baboons weren't. They were foraging. They must have decided that they were close enough to the campsite to be ready for action that night, as soon as Nyanya moved in for the kill. For the moment they were resting and feeding.

Sheena had to get them moving again; and they had to move in the right direction.

She had crept up on them silently. Even the guards had no idea she was there. This all had to be very skilfully managed.

Simply showing herself to them would not work. Yes, she could without doubt say enough rude things to them to get them to chase her, and she could lead them towards Nyanya. But she would not be able to outrun them over such a distance. They would catch her much too soon.

She retraced her steps to the river bank. From here she might have a chance. She would have to make sure they didn't actually see her before they got this far. She had to lay a trail.

So she set off back towards the baboons once more. This time she stopped every now and again and had a pee.

Now she was very precise about this. The contents of her bladder would have to last the whole distance. She was glad she had had that enormous drink.

Peeing would be too much, in fact. She could only afford to

piddle each time she stopped. So she ran a little, piddled a little, ran some more, piddled some more, back to where the baboons were. Before she got there she was only managing to widdle. By the time she reached the clearing she had run out.

'I'll have to wait a liddle,' she said to herself. So she hid in the shadow of a bush.

The young male baboons were patrolling as usual. She waited until one was coming directly towards her and squeezed out as much as she could. The best she could produce was a diddle. Then she slipped silently back through the shadows and away from the clearing. She stopped where she would be able to hear what happened.

There was a pause until the baboon reached the bush. Then she could hear him sniffing. Then he sniffed some more.

'Gwahoo!'

He'd smelt her.

'Gwahoo!' again, and the other males came pounding up.

'That cat thing! That spy! That creature! The one that insulted us and dropped the baby on its head! It's been here!'

'It must have come to warn the lion.'

'I'd like to get my teeth into its stumpy little tail! Did you see the way the nasty little cheat waggled it at us as it was flying off?'

Sheena didn't remember doing that, but wished she had thought of it.

'I'd like to sharpen my canines on its little backbone!'

That sounded like the baboon who had been in charge of the group that captured her.

'I'll crunch its little skull and scatter the splinters from the top of Ketabong Hill.'

That was the overall troop leader, who as the top politician had to come up with a big promise.

For once Sheena didn't mind being called little. The more the baboons saw as 'little' this animal who had outwitted them, the more likely they were to feel insulted again and whip themselves up into a fury which would drive them to chase her.

'Hunting party!'

That command was from the leader. It was all Sheena needed to hear. She was already far enough away to be able to scamper off without worrying about being heard, and in any case the male baboons made a lot of commotion as they got organised.

She ran as fast as she could towards the river bank.

She was out of breath by the time she got there, and she had left the baboons well behind. She was shocked, though, to see the sun sinking behind the trees. Was she in time?

The baboons would have to stop every now and again to scout around for the next smell patch, and as she laid her trail she had deliberately changed direction a couple of times to slow them down; but she had not wanted to slow them down too much. Had she done that?

Now she crossed over the sand onto the other side, and scrambled up onto a fallen tree so that she was in plain view. Nyanya was only fifty yards away around the next bend.

Soon she heard the baboons. They were calling to each other as they ran. Once or twice the sound stopped moving forward, then after more barking it got closer again.

Suddenly the baboons burst out through the trees on the opposite river bank. They saw her immediately and screamed in anger. Without pausing they ran down onto the river bed and started pounding across it towards her.

Started, then slowed, as their feet, small for the size and weight of their bodies, sank into the shifting sand. Sheena had been relying on that. She jumped down from the tree-trunk onto the hard ground of the bank and ran through the scrub towards Nyanya's bush, taking care to stay where the baboons would be able to see her. She could hear them struggling behind her. Once they reached the bank they would quickly catch up.

But she was soon there, at the bush.

Nyanya wasn't. The old lion had already left.

There was nothing for it but to carry on running. River bank or river bed? Which would help her keep ahead of the baboons the longer? Her paws were small also, and she knew she would soon tire in the sand…but if she stayed up on the bank and they followed her there, they would easily catch her. So she leapt down into the sand and began running.

The baboons changed direction and began pounding down the sand river after her. Once they got up speed, it seemed they had less trouble with the soft sand.

Sheena soon fully rounded the bend and reached the straight stretch at the end of which she had seen the children. For now she was out of sight of the baboons; but the sand was deep here, and her paws sank a long way into it so that she came almost to a halt. She was forced to jump back up onto the bank. It was quite high at this point and she had a good view of what lay ahead.

What lay ahead, and not too far ahead now, was the corner where Thomas and Amy had been digging. She could see the holes they had made in the sand; but she could not see them, nor anything blue, nor any sign of red.

There, however, there was Nyanya, crouching and creeping along under the left-hand bank, clearly trying to make no noise. She was stalking. She was stalking the children, Sheena knew. The children must be just a little way up the bank on the other side.

Nyanya *must* be hard of hearing, not to have noticed the turmoil behind her – even though the baboons had not barked or screamed for a while, probably because they needed all their breath for the chase. Sheena looked back. They were coming round the bend. They saw her. At the same time they saw Nyanya beyond her; and Nyanya stopped, turned and snarled at them all.

Everything depended on this moment. Which did they hate the more, the little cat or the Big Cat?

They had Sheena's scent in their nostrils and anger against her in their hearts, and there she was up on the bank, close to them. But there too was Nyanya, down where they were on the river bed, and Nyanya was a lion and they feared all lions and since fear and hate often go together they hated all lions also. Fear and hate are stronger than anger; and they might never get another chance like this.

But they turned towards Sheena.

They had set off to hunt her down and could think of nothing else. Anger and the needs of the moment got in the way of their deeper feelings.

They churned across the river bed, leapt up onto the bank and immediately began to gain on her. She had no choice but to jump down onto the sand in the hope that it would slow them down more than it slowed her.

She ran towards the bend where Nyanya was crouching.

But it was Sheena the baboons were chasing. They would catch her, and stop, and tear her, and Nyanya would get away…and come back later for Amy and Thomas. Nothing had been achieved.

Then suddenly the sand gave way under Sheena's front paws. Slip, slide, tumble, plop! She had fallen into an elephant water hole. The hole collapsed in on her. She was upside-down, buried in sand. (She had also fallen on her head.) Fortunately there was very little water in the bottom of the hole.

To the baboons it must have seemed as if she had simply vanished into thin air. That was the second time she had done something like that to them.

They did not even pause. As soon as she was out of sight she was out of mind. There, just over there, was that evil old lion trying to escape. Fear and hatred took over from anger. On! On!

Their 'On! On!' carried them straight over Sheena's hole. Their pounding feet stamped and tamped the heavy sand down on top of her. She had to wriggle a space for herself so that she could breathe, then twist around and dig and scrabble her way back up to the surface.

By the time she reached it and had shaken the sand out of her eyes and whiskers, Nyanya had almost reached the bend. The baboons were floundering after her, not gaining any ground (and not, luckily, paying any attention to the lumpy, sand-covered figure that had emerged behind them).

Nyanya's limp was obvious, and her age was obvious, and there was no knowing how long she would be able to keep running like that. She rounded the bend out of sight. The baboons followed, screaming in rage. The sand sprayed up as they turned the corner.

Sheena was left alone and forgotten among the deep and empty tracks of the chase.

The screaming became fainter and fainter until it could be heard no more.

Chapter Seventeen: Kwaheri

Sheena hoped Nyanya would survive. Everything had to die sooner or later, and not just in the wild; but often what mattered most was how it happened. The baboons would not offer an easy death.

What mattered more to Sheena now, however, was that she find Thomas and Amy.

That didn't take long. There was a faint track up from the river bed and she followed it. Soon she heard voices, and she knew them. She approached cautiously and came to a flat open space under some large trees. There was the Land Rover, there were the two green tents with the table and chairs in front of them, and there were the Allens.

Mum was being annoyed with the children.

'We told you not to be long. Dad was just about to come and get you…and we're very busy packing up.'

'And all that noise – what was it?'

That was Dad Allen's voice, from inside one of the tents. His khaki behind came out first through the tent door, followed by the rest of his body on its hand and knees.

'Baboons we think. They must have come down the river bed just after we left. We didn't see them but it sounded like they were very angry about something,' Thomas said.

One of the things the baboons had been very angry about was by now under a bush behind the tents.

'Have you sorted your bags out yet, like you were told to?' asked Mum.

Sheena was happy to be back close to the hurly-burly of family life.

'There were lots of great stones. Look!'

Thomas was trying the diverting trick.

'Have you packed your *bags*? Well, pack them. Shoo!'

Mum had not looked at what Thomas was trying to show her; and she had not needed to wait for an answer to her question. Amy and Thomas did not wait for her to repeat the command either: they knew when they had dawdled too long and had stretched things too far. They crawled into the tent nearer to Sheena and got busy. Sheena could hear Thomas muttering under his breath, however:

'Children who shilly-shally shouldn't be shamefully chivvied, shooed, chided or otherwise chastised.'

She sneaked over to one of the big trees overlooking the tents and climbed it. She found a comfortable spot where no-one would see her, and settled down to watch.

She watched all night. She did not expect any old lions to come nosing around the campsite, but...

She was still watching the next morning as the Allens had breakfast, pulled down the tents and packed away everything that was not already in the Land Rover.

While the family were loading she crept down the back of the tree trunk, walked down to the river bed, found another elephant water-hole, and had a long drink (taking care not to fall in). She needed that.

There were no animals around, and the only sign of what had happened the evening before was the churned-up sand.

There was more space in the Land Rover for the return

journey, and she had no difficulty stowing herself away without anyone seeing. Once the back doors had been slammed and the engine had roared into life, she was even able to crawl up onto the tent bag, which was much higher up this time but hidden from the passengers by the folding tables. Dad Allen had insisted they would be better standing upright and Mum had let him have his way. He had been a very good Chief Camper.

Sheena was very pleased at the thought that they would soon be heading back home, even though she knew how bumpy the road was going to be.

She was even more pleased as they pulled away from the campsite. Thomas called out, 'Sheena, here we come,' and Amy shouted, 'Good old Sheena!' She nearly crawled forward from her hiding place and did some Extreme Licking.

From on top of the tent bag Sheena could see out of one of the rear windows. As they drove towards the gate she watched the sandy track stretching away backwards and the trees shrinking. She was leaving a lot behind.

Then she noticed a large giraffe head looking over the top of a tall bush at the edge of the track. She knew he could see her.

'Bye, Twiga,' she said softly. 'Kwaheri!'

To one side of the bush was a much younger giraffe. She recognized him as well. She was pleased.

'Kwaheri, Baragandiri!' shouted Thomas as they swung out through the gate. Dad Allen, delighted to be back on the road in *Great White*, accelerated hard. The engine roared off as if it was going on ahead, and the Land Rover itself gradually caught up.

They were home in a trance. Sheena was stiff for days afterwards, though.

No-one ever knew she had been away. She got back into the house from the Land Rover as cleverly as she had got into the Land Rover from the house. So that when Thomas and Amy burst in through the front door ready to scoop her up in their arms and squeeze her, she was lying on the sofa, ready to act with her usual disdain. She allowed them only one squeeze each before she jumped down and stalked (a different kind of stalking) out through the door as if this affection was all too much, given the fact that she had been abandoned for six whole days.

By the next morning things were back to normal (except for Sheena's stiff joints and painful punctures, and her tail, which had a bit of grey mud still stuck to it).

Cats are Conservative. They like to keep things the way they are. That's usually because they've spent a lot of time getting them that way. When their way of life has been disturbed at all, they work hard to make sure it goes back to what it was. That is what Sheena did.

She decided she almost certainly wouldn't want to go on safari again. But she would never forget the frightening beauty of the leopard, the calmness of the raggedy lion's eyes, nor the smell of golden grass like a freshly-baked, crusty loaf.

However…

189

...you probably noticed that there are several places on the map (Pages 44 and 45) that didn't come into this story – Lake Salangani, for instance, and the Dimdarong Forest. That's because they have more to do with Sheena's next adventures in Baragandiri, which are described in *The Gradual Elephant*.

Then there are the Dry Highlands (look at the top left corner of the map). What happens there?

The Meerkat Wars happen there. They are terrifying; and Sheena finds herself in the middle of them...